"I'm Nora Chase from Keepsakes."

She held out the chic midnight-blue and silver shopping bag. "I've brought the gift you ordered."

David Sommer leaned against the door frame, looking down at her with a mixture of frustration, surprise and amusement, a potentially lethal combination in so attractive a man. "You're about three minutes too late, Ms Chase."

"Oh?"

"The lady for whom the gift was intended didn't stick around to receive it."

He didn't seem particularly devastated, and Nora was oddly relieved. "I'm sorry your evening didn't work out."

"It didn't . . . and it did. Diane and I weren't exactly made for each other." He was giving Nora the kind of look that said *she* had his full attention now. "Thanks for delivering the gift in person, Nora."

"Satisfied clients are Keepsakes's aim," she answered smoothly.

"Now there's a promising thought. . . ."

Madeline Harper's twentieth romance novel, *Keepsakes*, marks this fine writing team's tenth anniversary since joining forces in 1978. Longtime friends, both Madeline Porter and Shannon Harper work at other jobs apart from their writing; Madeline for a community theater and Shannon in a university library. And both absolutely *hate* to shop. "One of our fantasies," says Shannon, "is to have someone like our heroine, Nora, to do that chore for us."

Although the two halves of Madeline Harper live thousands of miles apart— Shannon in Georgia and Madeline in California—they are always with each other in thought. The team has also written under the pseudonym Anna James.

Books by Madeline Harper

HARLEQUIN TEMPTATION

Keepsakes
MADELINE HARPER

Harlequin Books

TORONTO • NEW YORK • LONDON
AMSTERDAM • PARIS • SYDNEY • HAMBURG
STOCKHOLM • ATHENS • TOKYO • MILAN

To Libby, with appreciation for her patience
and invaluable assistance

Published July 1988

ISBN 0-373-25310-9

Printed in U.S.A.

1

THE WOMEN'S VOICES played point-counterpoint across the room. Nora Chase, sitting at the Louis XIV table she used for a desk, spoke in a low, controlled voice. Only those who listened closely were able to detect the hint of a Southern accent that surfaced now and again.

In contrast, the accent of her assistant, Janice Lavette, was pure New Yorkese. Right now Janice was doing what she did best, brow-beating one of their suppliers.

"I know it's Friday, and I know you're booked," she said, gesturing excitably with her pencil as she negotiated with the delivery service. "But you can fit in one more pickup, can't you, Dan? It's nearby, within walking distance for your messenger." She didn't pause for comment but plunged ahead. "He won't even have to hassle for a cab. Just do me this favor," she prodded. "You owe me one, remember? Why? Well, I gave you those two great leads. Because of me you're getting richer and richer. You will? Great. I knew you'd see it my way. And Dan, get someone here before five, will ya?"

Only half listening to her own phone call, Nora watched with amusement as her assistant arranged herself more comfortably on the floor and made a notation on the pad that rested against her knees. Janice had always claimed that she did her best work cross-legged on the floor, especially when cajoling on the telephone. Nora had acquiesced as long as her assistant promised to sit in a chair when there were clients in the office.

Finally, her voice still calm and melodious, Nora made a concerted effort to put an end to her call. "I appreciate your interest, sir, but I must remind you again that Keepsakes has never dealt in such requests." She pushed her tortoiseshell glasses back into her hair and rolled her eyes heavenward, reiterating, "We're not involved in that kind of service. There's simply no way we could fill your order."

A long silence followed, after which Nora breathed a sigh of relief and said, "I think that's a wonderful idea. Australia would be just the place for you to begin the search. I'll let you go now so you can start on those overseas calls."

As Nora hung up, laughter took over, sparkling in her dark eyes. "I believe this is a Keepsakes first. He wanted me to find a koala bear and deliver it to his niece on her birthday!"

"That's weird, but I have a better one. A woman called this morning asking us to decide what her tropical fish would like for *its* birthday."

"I hope you told her we'd have to get to know the fish first."

"That's exactly what I told her, and she agreed."

Nora's smile lit her eyes again. Her face, usually lovely and poised, became suddenly playful, making her look far younger than her thirty-one years. It was a look reserved for close friends like Janice, rarely seen by her wealthy and chic clients, for whom Nora Chase was the epitome of elegance. "Didn't I promise that you'd never be bored if you came to work for me?"

Janice stood up, put a file folder on the desk and then plopped back down onto the floor, rearranging her legs in a lotus position. "It's hard to believe I've been here for three years, but I haven't been bored for a minute, not even a second. 'Course, I don't know how you managed that first year without me," she teased.

"Are you kidding? I couldn't afford you the first year. It was daring enough leaving the department store and going out on my own. When I finally moved to the West Side and hired you, I was scared to death, but I knew I had to be more 'professional.' A nice apartment and an assistant added to my image. Of course, I had no idea when I invested in a few pieces of antique furniture that you would spend most of your work day on the floor."

Janice giggled again. "But now look at us with more clients than we can handle, even though some of them are complete weirdos. If you'd advertise, or go on one of those talk shows that are so interested in Keepsakes, we really would be in clover."

"Nope," Nora declined. "That would bring in another kind of client, and we'd lose the special people, the ones who like the personal touch, the feeling that they're important."

"People like David Sommer?"

"Hmm," Nora evaded.

"What do you mean by 'hmm'?" Janice quizzed, not waiting for an answer as she declared, "he's one of our best accounts and definitely our most fascinating client."

"Janice, you've never met him." Nora's tone combined both surprise and reproach.

"I know, and neither, I might add, have you. That makes him even more intriguing."

Nora just shook her head and got back to work. There was more on her mind than David Sommer as she thumbed through the week's accounts, preparing them for the bookkeeper, who would be coming in the next day. It had been a good week—a good month, in fact. Nora still kept her fingers crossed, still had to pinch herself occasionally to believe that this business, which had started almost as a fluke, had caught on so well.

Just four years before, she'd been a personal shopper, running around from department to department in a huge store, coordinating outfits by beginning with the perfect dress, then adding a scarf and pin, just the right belt, shoes, earrings, all the accessories. The women who had sought her services had always been pleased, and some of them had begun to ask Nora for help with other items that weren't available in the store. Nora found herself moonlighting, specializing in getting to know her clients' tastes, making the ideal selection and soon choosing gifts for their families, friends, business associates, lovers.

The timing was perfect. She'd been at the right place at the right moment. Everything had worked for Nora—the busy, affluent members of society who were her clients, her own natural good taste and flair, and her exotic good looks. Tall and statuesque with dark hair and eyes, Nora dressed simply and elegantly in blacks, whites and beiges. Her style was never flamboyant; everything about her bespoke a chic that put her clients at ease. She was one of them. Yet she'd never quite gotten over her surprise at her success, and she'd never been able to take anything for granted.

"You know," Janice said, glancing up at Nora, who was still poring intently over the accounts, "it's time for a vacation. You haven't taken any time off all summer."

"I don't dare go away for more than a weekend for fear I'll return and it'll all be gone."

Janice looked at her boss closely, green eyes narrowed. "You're kidding, aren't you?"

Nora raised her eyebrows for a moment, thinking, and then answered with a shrug, "Sure, I'm kidding."

"Well, since I'm only an employee, I never have a moment's anxiety about my holiday. I just wish my two weeks hadn't come and gone."

"But it was a worthwhile holiday," Nora reminded her. "You met the current love of your life."

"You bet I did," Janice said with a grin. "And I have a date with Tom tonight. I'll have to leave early, so if our client arrives with her tropical fish—"

"Janice, please—"

"Just kidding. She's going to call first."

"So I get to come up with a birthday present for her aquatic pet?"

Janice shook her head. "I already had a great idea. A mini TV set. The only problem is rigging up something to attach it to the outside of the tank."

Before Nora could moan, Janice remembered the messenger pickup. "I got Dan to add an extra delivery today for that reception-room mirror. They'll be here before five."

"I bet that took some finagling."

"You're right. Dan was short of staff because of vacation and all that, but I mentioned one or two favors he owed us, and he agreed. It's only a few blocks, so I didn't tell him how heavy the mirror is. All his messengers are big and burly, anyway."

"I don't know what we'd do if Dan didn't have a crush on you," Nora said.

"Unfortunately, he's never gotten around to asking me out, so I've had to settle for Tom," she bemoaned but with a teasing smile. "Here are today's orders for you to look over."

"Yes, ma'am," Nora said demurely, pulling her glasses down to the tip of her nose and perusing the list.

She was familiar with the clients' needs, having worked with all of them before. Nora's clients included the famous and near famous, the movers and shakers, names in the headlines as well as many who carefully avoided the limelight. There was the occasional business executive who needed presents for his associates, the actress who wanted to give special gifts when her show closed, the hostess whose house-party guests expected mementos.

Recently, she'd begun to get requests from people who didn't fit into a top echelon category at all, and her business had broadened to include the elderly and homebound who couldn't shop for themselves and even children who'd saved their money conscientiously and wanted to remember their parents' birthdays. In every case, they called on Nora to help them, which she did, quickly and seemingly without effort.

It wasn't effortless, of course. Nora worked long hours, often seven days a week. When she'd told Janice she was afraid to stop and rest, there had been more truth to her words than jest. Nora knew the world of the rich and privileged; she'd lived for years on the outside looking in. Now she was on its periphery, but not without sacrifice. Her struggle to establish Keepsakes had been a lonely one filled with transitory pleasures and other people's satisfactions. She'd had little time for anything but work, less time to let anyone into her personal life.

That's why Janice had become more than an assistant to her. She was Nora's closest friend in New York. They worked well together, joking at times and at other times, such as now, working quietly in companionable silence, a team that had made Keepsakes the top personalized shopping service in New York.

"What time is your date?" Nora asked, breaking the silence as she put her list aside.

"Six o'clock," Janice answered.

"Then you better get going. The Friday afternoon traffic is always hellacious."

"I'm just closing things down here." Janice struggled to her feet, stacking notes on the desk as the doorbell and phone rang simultaneously. "You take the call," she advised, "and I'll get the door." She glanced at her watch as she walked down the hall toward the foyer. "That'll be the messenger, and he's right on time. Old Dan came through again."

Nora was still on the phone when Janice returned, scooped up all her papers from the floor, filed some away and tossed the others. Seemingly satisfied, she plopped her sunglasses on top of her head, slung her bag over her shoulder and started for the door.

Nora sent her off with a goodbye wave but noticed the next time she looked up that her assistant was still there, standing in the doorway, blatantly listening to the telephone conversation, which was not a pleasant one for Nora; in fact, it was beginning to irritate her. She tried to stay calm and treat the caller as she treated all her customers, with interest and respect. It wasn't easy.

The voice on the other end was authoritative and demanding. "I've always been able to count on Keepsakes in the past. Why not now?"

"I'm sorry, Mr. Sommer," Nora responded, "but you've given me very short notice. I don't see how I can have a gift delivered by eight o'clock tonight."

Although the client's comeback was low-key, in its casualness there was a demand that was unspoken but obvious. "I thought service and dependability were your trademarks, Ms Chase. If I can't count on you when I need you . . ."

His voice drifted off, but Nora caught the implied threat: in the future he might not use her service as frequently, if at all. She looked up at Janice, forming a moue of dismay with her lips. All she got in return from her assistant was a wicked little smile that she could have done without.

"What is it that you need?" Nora asked her caller, hoping for a request so impossible that a refusal would be unquestioned.

"A farewell gift for a young lady. We're having dinner, and I want to present it to her then."

"Is she leaving the country? Going on holiday?" Nora's mind worked quickly—luggage, an elegant travel case.

"No, just out of my life."

Unexpected spots of anger flamed in Nora's cheeks. She turned her head slightly so that Janice wouldn't notice. It wasn't often that she allowed her assistant to see her flustered, but Nora couldn't help it this time. Her other clients didn't use Keepsakes to pay people off. Nora believed this one did. Today the recipient of David Sommer's largesse was a woman, apparently a girlfriend or, it now appeared, an ex-girlfriend.

Even though she was irritated by the demand, it wasn't her place to comment on a client's behavior, and Nora was a pro. "All right," she said, "I'll see what I can do."

"An appropriate gift," he stressed, "by eight o'clock."

"Of course, Mr. Sommer."

Nora hung up the phone with more than customary care. She'd been struggling to maintain control. She'd succeeded and was able to look up at Janice—who hadn't ventured from her spot in the doorway—with a smile. "David Sommer," she said.

"I gathered. Our A-number-one customer. Who's the outrageous architect bestowing gifts on this time? His entire staff? The wives of all his business associates?"

"No."

"Everyone at Shea Stadium? The entire cast of the Met?"

Nora couldn't help laughing, but she sobered quickly. "Just one gift, for a lady. A farewell present, as a matter of fact."

Janice's eyes grew large. "What woman would be crazy enough to exit his life?"

"I must remind you again, Janice, that you don't know the man."

"But I know *about* him, and I saw his picture in a gossip magazine. He's incredibly handsome, the kind of guy who's definitely my type. Rich, of course, and, judging from his voice, definitely sexy."

"That's obviously a practiced voice," Nora said, not admitting that she'd thought the same thing, even today when what he'd said hadn't charmed her in the slightest. And charm was what he had the most of. She tried to convey that to the mischievous Janice.

"David Sommer is a man who thinks he can buy anything or anyone, solve any problem by sending a gift, usually at the last minute, always with the demand for perfection. That kind of man doesn't interest me remotely. He's all surface charm and nothing else."

"But he's a good client," Janice reminded her.

"Yes, he is that. Fortunately most of my other clients aren't cut in the same mold. If I had to deal with people like him all day, I'd close up and return to the department store. By the way," Nora added, "why are you still here? I believe you mentioned a six o'clock date, didn't you?"

"Yep, but I couldn't resist hearing what David had to say."

"So it's 'David' now?"

"Well, I've talked to him on the phone almost weekly for the past two years. I like to refer to him as 'David,' to think of him as 'David,' to dream—"

"Well, you keep dreaming while I rush around in the ninety-degree heat finding a gift for Mr. Sommer's soon to be ex-girlfriend."

"I just feel awful about leaving," Janice said with a grin.

"No, you don't, and I certainly can't blame you. Now go. I'll see you Monday. And have fun," she called to Janice's retreating back.

"You do the same," Janice trilled over her shoulder as she headed merrily down the hall.

THE REST OF NORA'S DAY definitely didn't fall into the classification of fun. Many of the small specialty shops she depended upon were closed, their owners having taken off early on Friday for weekends in the Hamptons. She finally had to go all the way across town to find what she wanted in a little antique shop on Second Avenue.

The music box was French and old. It was also very
expensive, but Nora didn't care about that in the least,
and she knew David Sommer wouldn't, either. Since
the first time he'd called on Keepsakes, at the recom-
mendation of a friend, he'd never asked the price or
complained when the bill was sent.

This time Nora expected she would get a diabolical
sense of pleasure from sending him the bill, adding a
hefty fee that would reflect the outside temperature.

It was still hovering at ninety degrees, and the pavement hadn't cooled off in the least; in fact, Nora could
actually feel the heat coming up through her shoes from
the sizzling sidewalks. It didn't help when she had to
walk all the way to Lexington Avenue in her search for
a cab, then give up in frustration and pile onto a bus
with hordes of people just as hot and irritable as she.

Half an hour later, Nora collapsed in her air-
conditioned apartment and called the delivery service.
Dan had gone, and the night dispatcher was pleasant
but firm; there was no way they could deliver David
Sommer's package by eight o'clock.

After trying half a dozen other services with no success, Nora was left with two choices: to deliver the gift
herself or to call David Sommer and tell him she was
unable to fill his request. Before that second choice was
a completed thought, she knew it wasn't possible. She'd
built Keepsakes not only on flair and originality but on
dependability and service. No, she'd have to brave the
heat again.

Nora wasn't sure why he irritated her so much, but
as she sat in the cab on her way to his apartment, she

decided that it was mainly his assumption that every-one would do as he asked. Well, in this case, acquies-cence was only fair, since she was in the business of satisfying her clients. Somehow, with the others, even the difficult ones, she didn't mind. Nora had devel-oped with each of them a mutual trust and liking.

She'd always felt it was necessary to get to know the people she worked for on a personal basis to better un-derstand their needs, their tastes. All her regular clien-tele had been to her office-apartment, or she'd visited with them in their homes in order to establish a rap-port, except for one couple who lived abroad. The duke and duchess, still holding on to their titles, roamed the Continent. Nora talked to them via transatlantic phone calls and mailed their gifts to whatever part of the world they happened to be in at the time, but she'd never met them.

And she'd never met David Sommer. Yet it was clients like him—with frequent requests, capricious, demanding and willing to pay—who kept the business going and allowed her to work with others whose needs were less flamboyant and spectacular. That was why she was on her way uptown at that moment.

Nora took advantage of the creeping traffic to repair the damage the past few hours had wreaked upon her. She pulled out her hand mirror, took one long look and wondered if repair was possible. She really needed to start all over. Her clothes looked as though they'd just come out of a washing machine, her stockings felt like iron casings around her legs, and her hair, well, it drooped across her face with a will of its own.

Fortunately her all-cotton outfit was supposed to have a rumpled look, although today it gave a new meaning to the word. She dabbed at her makeup, brushed her hair and added a little lip gloss. As the cab deposited her at David Sommer's co-op, Nora wondered why in the world she was bothering, and told herself it was habit. Appearance was important in her work, and David Sommer was, after all, a good customer.

Nora crossed the lobby just as the elevator doors slid soundlessly open and one of the loveliest women she'd ever seen emerged. She was tall with tawny blond hair that fanned out from her face like a mane. Her eyes were sea green; her earrings were emerald. She wore a green jersey tunic and one of the most self-satisfied smiles Nora had ever seen. Her high heels barely made a sound as she crossed the marble-tiled floor.

Looking after the woman, Nora couldn't help but be intrigued. She seemed so proud and confident, as beautiful as she was pleased with herself. Maybe, Nora thought, she, too, would emerge from the elevator on David Sommer's floor transformed into a cool, collected and self-confident woman. Then she thought again. She'd get off looking exactly the same, hot and tired after traipsing all over town. After all, elevators couldn't work magic. The woman she'd seen had been born with that look.

Yet when she stepped off the elevator and caught a glimpse of herself in the hall mirror, she was surprised to see a look that was at least presentable. Maybe it was magic, after all. With that thought turning her lips into a smile, she rang the bell of David Sommer's apartment.

Even before the door opened, he was talking. "Diane," he said, "you're back—"

"I'm Nora Chase from Keepsakes." Nora held out the chic midnight-blue-and-silver shopping bag that was one of Keepsakes' trademarks. "I've brought the gift you ordered."

She couldn't read the look on David Sommer's face, for even though he hadn't introduced himself, there was no mistaking who he was. Everything about him looked expensive, his clothes, his haircut, even his tan, which made his eyes a blue that wasn't quite believable. He was long and lean and, as Janice had predicted, very handsome.

He leaned against the doorframe, looking down at her with a mixture of frustration, surprise and amusement. "Well, well, Ms Chase. You're just about three minutes too late."

"I'm sorry. The traffic on Friday is unbelievable." She tried to apologize without sounding defensive. If he only knew what she'd been through during the past couple of hours.

"It's not your fault," he said in a voice still slightly bemused. "This little fiasco rests totally on me." He looked at her again, more carefully this time, and a smile lit his face and his eyes as if he very much liked what he saw. "Come in," he said, "and cool off. I imagine it's still hot as a furnace outside." He stood in front of floor-to-ceiling windows that looked out on Central Park. "I'm sure you could use a cool drink."

There was no doubt about that. Nora asked for sparkling water with lots of ice and then turned to admire David Sommer's panoramic view. Before she could take it in, she noticed a table beautifully set for two. The candles were lit, the china and silverware sparkled, the champagne was on ice and beside one of the plates there was an elegantly wrapped gift.

Confusion darkened Nora's eyes, and her business side bristled. "It seems you already bought a gift, Mr. Sommer. I hope this doesn't indicate a lack of confidence in my ability." She tried to keep her voice soft and low, but a little tremor of anger shook it when she thought about her hot afternoon's work to satisfy his whim, all her effort, it appeared, unnecessary.

His back was to her as he fixed their drinks at the bar. Raising her voice, she asked, "Did you suppose I wouldn't complete your job?"

David turned then and gave Nora her drink. A freshly cut lemon slice perched on the edge of the tall, frosty glass. He walked over to the table and, with a total lack of interest, looked down at the package.

"This," he said, raising one eyebrow, "is not a gift from me—it's a gift *to* me."

He gestured toward the cream-colored sofa. "Please have a seat. I feel so bad that you made this trip for nothing."

For nothing. Perplexed, Nora sat down.

He went back to the bar and poured himself a Scotch on the rocks. The look of frustration and surprise had gone from his eyes, but the amusement remained. Seeing that Nora was still confused, he explained. "The woman for whom my gift was intended didn't wait around for it. In fact, I didn't even get to make the speech to go with my presentation of the lovely—" He looked at Nora.

"French music box."

David smiled. "French music box." The smile created a deep cleft in each cheek and revealed straight, even teeth that were porcelain white against his tanned skin. "Unfortunately," he continued, "my friend Diane got a hint that tonight was going to be farewell and took matters into her own hands." He picked up the elaborately beribboned box from the table and then put it down again. "A farewell gift to me."

He took a swig of his drink and grinned engagingly at Nora. "You know, I don't think this has ever happened to me before."

I'll bet it hasn't, Nora thought. She tried to look sympathetic but couldn't control the smile that teased the corners of her mouth. "Diane," she said hesitantly. "Is she blond?"

"Yes, that's Diane. Or that *was* Diane, blond and tall and not my type. Obviously," he joked.

Nora had to laugh at that. "I believe I saw her leaving the building." She didn't add that Diane had looked as though she'd enjoyed every minute of her farewell episode with David, but she was very, very tempted. Instead she sipped her drink and remarked, "I'm so sorry your evening didn't work out, Mr. Sommer."

"Well, it did and it didn't," he admitted, sitting down beside Nora on the sofa.

He was more handsome than Janice had described or probably even imagined. Nora found herself unreasonably interested in the scenario before her, David Sommer and his breakup with the lovely Diane.

He seemed more than willing to tell her all about it. "We both knew the end was coming," he said with a grin. "I guess it was a matter of which one of us made the first move."

"Had you been going together for a long time?" Nora couldn't believe she was asking such a question, but she was definitely intrigued.

"No," he said quickly. "We met at a party a couple of months ago and we've been going to parties ever since. In fact, that's about all we did." He grinned again. "It wasn't a very realistic relationship."

Nora nodded, her face ostensibly serious, but David was sure he saw amusement dancing in her dark eyes. Well, why not. It was amusing, this situation with Diane, totally meaningless, and both of them had known it. She'd been taken with the image he portrayed, that of bon vivant, man about town, high roller. David had conveniently fitted himself into that image since it was a comfortable one, but there were other parts of his life that Diane never saw, didn't care about. They were special and still private; no one had had a look at them yet. No one seemed to care about them, and sometimes David wondered if they were real or not. Maybe the surface part of him had taken over.

He shook away the thought. There was still a man in there somewhere who needed another kind of woman. Like Nora, perhaps? She certainly didn't resemble any of the other women who'd been in his life recently. She was unique looking but not model pretty like Diane. When he'd greeted her at the door her face had been flushed from the heat, but she looked totally cool now, like a young woman who'd stepped out of a Renaissance painting, regal, calm and yes, really quite beautiful.

He remembered how distant and businesslike she'd been on the phone, not at all eager to do as he'd asked. Now that he'd dragged her across town, her gift was going unappreciated. That wasn't the way to impress Nora Chase, and suddenly he wanted to impress her.

"I really do apologize Ms Chase—Nora," he corrected, looking for and receiving approval to call her by her first name. "I feel as though I know you from all our telephone conversations."

"You usually deal with my assistant," she corrected. Her words were cool, but there was an underlying hint of warmth, a honeyed softness in her voice.

"But you're Keepsakes, Nora. Your taste, your style go into each gift."

"Including a French music box that's going begging." She made a move to stand up, but David was on his feet first.

"I requested the gift, and you supplied it. Naturally, I intend to pay for the service as usual. If you'll just give me the bill, I'm sure someone I know will like it."

"Oh, I have no doubt about that," Nora said easily.

Frowning a bit at the import of her words, he took a checkbook out of the desk.

Seeing that he was waiting, Nora said, "I haven't figured out the commission yet." She worked over the sums in her head.

"Add a bonus for all the extra time," he reminded her, "and just give me a ballpark figure."

"How about a million dollars?" she asked with a smile.

He came within a hairsbreadth of telling her it was worth almost that much to have the pleasure of her company. But he caught himself and held off until she named a very fair price, after which he wrote the check.

Moving closer to give it to her, he noticed the faint, elusive scent of her perfume. Elusive. That was it, just like Nora. He saw then that her eyes, which he'd thought were brown, were really hazel with flecks of green and gold in them. They were wonderful eyes, eyes a man could lose himself in forever.

She reached for the check, but he held on to it for just a fraction of a moment. He didn't want her to leave, not yet. He'd almost forgotten why she'd come. "Again, my apologies."

"That's quite all right, Mr. Sommer."

So, he thought, it was still "Mr. Sommer." Well, let her be formal; he wouldn't be. He wouldn't let her slip away, either. She was here and fascinating and he wanted to know more about her. He gestured toward the table. "Would you join me, Nora?"

The look on Nora's face gave nothing away, just a slight narrowing of the eyes, a raising of the eyebrows.

Under her scrutiny, David found himself talking much too rapidly. "After all, the table is set, the candles are lit, there's roast duck warming in the oven, and I want you to stay." Hearing the insistence in his voice, David quickly added, "Maybe dinner will make up for the inconvenience I've put you through." Nora didn't respond immediately, and he found himself flirting a little. "We really should get to know each other, don't you think, after our long telephone relationship?" He let himself linger on that final word, adding a little intimacy to it. He was doing well, David thought.

Nora apparently thought otherwise. "That's very thoughtful of you, Mr. Sommer, but it's been a long, hot day." She'd taken the check, folded it neatly and placed it in her lizard-skin purse.

She was aloof and distant and very lovely, with none of Diane's show-business good looks and probably none of her devotion to high living. But she wasn't very cooperative.

"To tell you the truth," she said, "I'm looking forward to the cool bath that's waiting for me a few blocks south of here."

David hid his disappointment with an understanding smile. He wasn't about to grovel, but her next words challenged.

"I'm sure you won't have any trouble finding another dinner date." She glanced toward the table that now seemed rather sad looking and held out her hand. "Thanks for your business, Mr. Sommer."

Determined that there'd be more than business between them, David was right behind her as Nora turned and walked toward the door.

"You'll be hearing from me soon," he said.

"Satisfied clients are Keepsakes' aim," she answered smoothly.

"I won't be calling as a client, Nora. I'll be calling to ask you to dinner."

Nora turned and looked at him for an instant just before she went out the door and it closed behind her. There had been no response. He hadn't expected one, but he didn't feel thwarted in the least.

"Oh, yes, Nora," he said aloud. "We will have dinner. I can promise you that."

2

"GOOD MORNING, Mr. Sommer." The receptionist flashed a smile that David returned as he pushed through the glass doors into the offices of Sommer International.

"Good morning, David."

"Good morning, Mr. Sommer."

The greetings of his staff followed him down the hall, and he acknowledged each one as he kept walking without breaking stride until he reached the corner office, shed his jacket and got down to work.

David Sommer rarely stopped working, and he'd imbued his employees with the same kind of driving energy and enthusiasm. Outsiders might think of him as demanding, but not those who worked for Sommer International. They found his quest for excellence an exciting challenge. He took an active interest in every aspect of the company, never asking more of the others than he was willing to give. David Sommer was everywhere at once. That was his style, and his co-workers respected him for it.

The architectural firm had a worldwide reputation, its projects not only financially successful but award winning. His speciality was the renovation of buildings, entire city blocks, whole neighborhoods. "Gentrification" was not even in his vocabulary; he left that to the hacks. The Sommer plan was more humane. Beginning in the earliest stages, in conference with city and local officials, he designed a blend of units that allowed new money in but didn't drive original residents out.

The success of the Sommer plan was staggering, and other architects had begun to imitate him in their renderings. That suited David fine. He had more work than he could handle, and he was proud to see his ideas take root all across the city. The buildings that grew from those roots were for everyone to share.

Beauty played a big part in his plans. He always insisted that his projects, whether public housing or corporate headquarters, be pleasing to the eye. For David Sommer was a man who appreciated beauty in all forms, which may have accounted for the fact that, after two long meetings and an hour of hard work at his drawing board, he poured another cup of coffee and thought about Nora Chase. Now *she* was a beautiful woman. Different, challenging, frustrating, but beautiful.

Since the hot Friday afternoon when they'd first met, he'd thought about her often—over a long weekend in Bar Harbor and a business trip to London. His thoughts were unbidden, unexpected but not unexplained.

Back in New York, he'd begun a telephone assault, calling every day and asking her out. Every day she refused, firmly, politely but maybe not irrevocably. He was determined to see her again, and he didn't mind subterfuge. Recently he'd tried a new tack. He would try it again.

Picking up the phone, he buzzed his secretary. "Get Keepsakes for me please, Maggie."

Moments later Maggie informed him, "Nora Chase is out of the office, boss."

"Is her assistant there?"

"Negative, but the answering service says she's expected soon," came the helpful reply. "Shall I call back?"

"No, thanks, Maggie. I'll try Janice myself in a few minutes."

Thank God for Janice Lavette, David thought as he waited, drumming impatient fingers on his desktop. For some reason she seemed to be on his side and had become an indispensable ally in his pursuit of Nora.

It had started when he'd first realized that Janice was perfectly willing to divulge her boss's whereabouts, and if Janice wasn't around, she passed orders on to the service. Apparently Nora liked her clients to be able to reach her wherever she was; that was part of the Keepsakes image, availability to meet anyone's needs at any time. His needs hadn't been exactly businesslike, but David had taken advantage of the Keepsakes philosophy.

He'd managed to track her down twice. The first time had been in a little antique shop in Soho, quite a distance from his office but easy to manage on a morning when there'd been a break in his usual activity. He'd cornered her between two Hepplewhite tables and hadn't given her time to be surprised.

"I wonder if you'd care to join me for lunch?" he asked casually, as if they hadn't just bumped into each other in the most unlikely place.

"Mr. Sommer," she said sotto voce, "I'm with clients."

David looked around and spotted an older couple, well dressed and attractive. "You're having lunch with them?"

"No, but—"

"Then I'll wait until you're free," he said adamantly. He and Nora were standing very close, necessarily because the aisles in the cramped shop were so narrow. David could hear the soft rhythm of her breathing, see her breasts rise and fall beneath her cream-colored silk dress.

"That may take some time, Mr. Sommer," she responded, causing David to suppress a smile. He was still "Mr. Sommer" to her; she would remain "Nora" to him. "When my clients leave—"

"We'll have lunch."

"No," she said. "I'll continue shopping for them. Now if you'll excuse me, I *am* working, as you can see, and must get back."

With that she tried to squeeze past him, but David made the maneuver as difficult as possible. He didn't move away, and their bodies touched in several intimate places, causing a smile to light his face and a blush to tint hers.

The next encounter had been only two days ago. Again, she'd been with a client, having lunch at a small Upper West Side restaurant. David and one of his staff had just happened to be at the next table, thanks to Janice's willingness to divulge anything and everything.

Nora had managed to ignore him during the meal, but David had waited her out, and luck was with him. The woman lunching with Nora had been called away to the telephone. That's when David had made his move, slipping into the vacated seat.

"I won't keep you but a moment," he said, noticing Nora's uneasy look. "This is all business. I need a special gift, one that only Keepsakes can provide for me." He kept his voice serious, remembering that teasing had gotten him nowhere in the past.

"And you need it by eight tonight?"

So it was her turn to tease, he thought, and decided to keep playing it straight. "In fact, I need it in about two weeks. I know you aren't fond of last-minute requests."

"That's very thoughtful, Mr. Sommer. What exactly are you looking for?"

David ran a hand through his thick hair and tried to keep his voice believable. This was the touchy part. "Actually, it'll take some time to explain."

"Mr. Sommer..."

Obviously she didn't believe a word he was saying, but David persisted. "If you'd just meet me for coffee, say, tomorrow morning."

"I'm sure you can describe your needs right now, Mr. Sommer, and eliminate another meeting."

"No, I can't," David said, "because your luncheon companion is about to reclaim her seat." David stood up politely, introduced himself to Nora's client and said in his most businesslike manner, "Then I'll call and make arrangements with your assistant for us to discuss the purchase, Ms Chase. And I'll see you tomorrow morning, if that's convenient."

Nora nodded curtly but didn't answer. As he walked back to his table, David heard the other woman saying, "What a handsome man. I hope the two of you have plans that are beyond the realm of business." He cringed at the words; they could only irritate Nora more, considering the mood she was in.

Apparently he'd been right. The following day, according to Janice, Nora had had no free time at all.

Well, this was a new day, and if Janice was back in the office, he was about to put an end once and for all to Nora's maddening elusiveness.

Picking up the phone, he dialed the Keepsakes number, which he now knew by heart, and told Janice, breathless from a dash from door to phone, to set up a meeting between him and Nora for noon the next day, at a café near his office.

"Why did you let him con you into that?" Nora demanded of her assistant later that afternoon.

Janice was unruffled. "He wants to discuss a purchase."

"He can discuss it with you."

Janice shook her head. "Unfortunately for me, that's not what David has in mind."

Nora shed her jacket and hung it over the back of a bentwood chair in the corner. "I told him only a few days ago that we can easily talk about his gift on the phone." She sank down onto the sofa.

"His request is quite unusual. He needs to show you exactly what he wants, describe it in person."

"Fine. Let him describe it to you."

"Like I said before, he wants *you*, Nora."

Nora laughed. "I'm sure he does, and it's not a meeting he wants. It's a lunch date."

"Oh, no," Janice contradicted. "He already has a one o'clock lunch, and he's meeting you for coffee earlier. That was very definite."

"And you believed it, of course." Nora shook her head and considered smiling, but she was still too annoyed.

"Of course," Janice declared. "I'm sure I didn't make a mistake, either, Nora. He has a very special gift in mind, and whatever it is really does require a personal meeting. I'd be willing to make a small wager to that effect," Janice added.

"I'm not about to gamble on this, Janice. Mr. Sommer is too clever for me to bet against. And too persuasive," she added, looking over the top of her glasses at her assistant.

"I guess it's the voice," Janice admitted. "I'm just a sucker for whatever it is that man's got."

Nora moved from the comfortable sofa over to the straight chair at her desk, willing herself to get back to work and discontinue this ridiculous conversation. But she knew what kind of voice it was, even though she wasn't about to discuss it with Janice. It was the kind of voice that commanded executives to drop what they were doing and pay attention, the kind that got the best seats on airplane flights, the best tables in restaurants, hotel reservations when there were no rooms available. It was also the voice that seduced beautiful women into just about anything he wanted, Nora imagined, but it wasn't going to seduce her.

"You admitted he was great looking," came Janice's comment from across the room.

Nora looked off into space and spoke as if to some unseen presence. "Sometimes I think separate offices would be a good idea, one for me and one for my assistant."

Janice wasn't in the least offended, and she wasn't about to let up. However, Nora managed to ignore her, for the rest of the day, at least.

THE NEXT MORNING, her assistant picked up where she'd left off. "I think he really likes you," Janice declared as the time approached noon and Nora prepared to leave.

"Wait a minute," Nora said, looking in the mirror where she'd stopped to check her makeup. "Weren't you just assuring me yesterday that this meeting the two of you arranged was business only?"

"Oh, it will be, the meeting this morning, in any case. I'm just talking in general."

"What about in general?"

"He likes you, obviously. He's been chasing you all over town trying to corner you long enough to have lunch. I call that attentive."

Nora added a little blush to her cheeks. "Not so, friend. He has something to prove by getting me to go out with him."

Janice, having settled onto the floor for her morning's work, looked up at Nora. "Like what?"

"Remember the night I met him?" Without waiting for a response, Nora went on. "He'd just been dumped, unceremoniously so, by a woman he'd planned to break up with. And I was a witness to that."

"So?"

"It's patently clear. He has to recapture that feeling of male superiority. I witnessed his defeat. Therefore he needs to charm me—however briefly."

Janice stared at Nora for a long time before she spoke. "I know you're older than I—and smarter and more mature, more savvy, more sophisticated...."

Nora was laughing. "Enough of the flattery. Get to the point."

"You're reasoning is the strangest I've ever heard. He's not trying to prove anything at all. The guy just likes you. Accept that, Nora."

Nora took another long look at herself in the mirror and then turned away quickly. She looked presentable; there was no reason to go to any further lengths for David Sommer. "Men like Mr. Sommer," she said, "have something to prove to themselves, to the world and, most important, to their egos. I understand David Sommer very well. He's used to getting what he wants, even if he has to pay a very high price."

Janice leaned against the desk, hands pressed against her temples. "This is all too complicated for me. I thought he was just a good-looking, rich man with a sexy voice."

"Well, he's definitely all those things," Nora admitted, "but obviously he's a man with an image to protect." She smiled wickedly at herself in the mirror. "He'd probably delight in having me fall madly in love with him so he could give *me* a farewell gift someday."

"Oh, Nora," Janice moaned, "all he wants is to meet you for a cup of coffee."

"I know, and I'm just being dramatic . . . and teasing you a little, but at least now that we're finally going to sit down together, maybe he'll stop following me all around town."

Janice giggled.

"What exactly was that for?" Nora asked, turning away from the mirror again, but not without tucking a wandering strand of hair back into place.

Janice stopped giggling to answer. "If you're impervious to his charms and attentions, then why are you taking so much time with your makeup?"

If Nora was thrown off base, she tried not to show it. "Because I want to present as favorable an image of Keepsakes as possible. We have a reputation to uphold, Janice."

Janice thought about that for a moment and then grinned impishly. "Pardon me for stepping out of line, but as my old grandaddy used to say, 'that's all a lot of bull.'"

The phone rang, and Janice picked it up quickly, thereby saving herself from her boss's wrath. "Keepsakes, may I help you?" she said before waving to Nora and mouthing the words, "Give David my love."

On her way to meet David Sommer, watching the familiar buildings pass by the cab window, Nora caught sight of a sign outside a newly completed structure. It declared in bold letters and no uncertain terms that the architect had been Sommer International. She let her glance climb skyward, craned her neck as they passed and then turned to look again out the back window.

It was a beautiful edifice, Nora admitted, not one of the modern monstrosities that were beginning to ruin New York's skyline, but a structure that fitted right into the architectural design of the older surrounding buildings. It was new and old at the same time and very, very beautiful. Well, why not, Nora asked herself, trying not to get carried away. David Sommer liked beauty, as witness the blond and very beautiful Diane.

Five minutes early for her rendezvous, Nora paused in the doorway, took off her huge dark glasses and let her eyes adjust to the light. She'd passed by the little Second Avenue café many times on peripatetic jaunts into this part of town for her clients, but she'd never even paused to look inside. She was delighted by what she saw. There was an Old World charm to the little café that she didn't associate with someone like David Sommer, but as Janice had begun to tell her, loudly and frequently, she really didn't know him.

She'd expected to be kept waiting and had even considered being late herself, but that wasn't Nora's way. No matter what, she was always on time for appointments. To her surprise, David was already there, seated at a table in the corner of the darkly paneled room.

He got up and came toward her, a handsome man, Nora had to admit once more. His lightweight suit fitted his athletic frame perfectly, and the blue of his broadcloth shirt set off the intense blueness of his eyes.

"Nora, I'm so pleased you were able to join me." There was a twinkle in his eye that they both knew reflected the conniving he'd gone through to get her there. Nora managed to ignore it by returning a look that was totally professional. He reached for her hand with both of his, but she was able to turn even that grasp into a businesslike handshake.

He pretended not to notice as he led her to the table, pulled out a chair and seated her. "I hope you like Darcy's," he said, taking his seat opposite her. "It's not trendy by any means, which is a welcome change, I think."

"You're absolutely right," Nora had to admit as she looked around at the room with its dark walls, soft lighting, profusion of plants and stained glass.

"Would you like an espresso?" David asked.

"No, thanks, not in this heat. Iced coffee, I think."

"A great idea." David signaled the waiter and placed their order before turning back to Nora, his eyes obviously enjoying what he saw but trying not to reveal that enjoyment. He didn't let it show in his voice, either.

"I'm so glad you could meet with me, Nora, because the purchase I want you to make for me is very important, and I needed the chance to explain it to you personally."

David's smile couldn't hide the pleasure he felt. She smiled back, but hers was of the lets-get-on-with-it variety.

The waiter arrived with their coffee, and Nora took a sip before getting down to business. "Tell me about this special gift, Mr. Sommer. What can I get for you?"

David didn't pause, didn't skip a beat. "A llama," he said.

The impossible request, the one that would be so easy to turn down. Nora felt relief and the urge to laugh. Instead she shook her head and responded, "I'm sorry, Mr. Sommer, but Keepsakes has a very strict policy. Never under any circumstances do we deal in live animals. You'll have to get your llama somewhere else." Trying to be helpful, she added, "I'm sure Janice would be glad to research this for you and come up with names of people who might be able to help."

David looked steadily back at her. "No, Nora, I must insist that *you* help me with the llama."

Nora did laugh then, with relief. "I'm afraid that's not possible. We wouldn't break our rule for anyone, not even you."

He looked across the table at her and let himself enjoy what he saw this time, slowly take it all in. She was wearing another simple but stylish outfit, a suit of beige linen. She seemed to prefer soft, natural colors and materials, and today she'd added a blouse of palest green silk. Her dark hair was pulled back from her oval-shaped face, and her unusual eyes seemed larger than he'd remembered. She looked like a million dollars, and David couldn't help but feel a little smug that he'd finally talked her into this meeting. Of course, here she was after ten minutes, ready to refuse him, get up and walk out. But that wasn't going to happen.

"Not a live llama," he informed Nora. "A jeweled llama pin." David thought he noticed a trace of disappointment in Nora's eyes when she realized she wasn't going to be able to refuse him, after all. Quickly he took a note pad and pen from his suit pocket and began sketching.

"I'd like something about this size."

Nora put on her glasses and looked at the sketch. "About two inches high?"

"No more than that. She's a very petite woman."

Nora cast a sidelong glance at him but kept her thoughts to herself.

"I'd like it jeweled, of course, multicolored, perhaps, or possibly just one kind of stone. I'll leave that to you. Naturally I'd prefer an antique pin, but I know that might not be possible. Whatever you find, it's not to be costume jewelry. I don't want anything fake."

"I didn't imagine that you would," Nora said as she studied the drawing he'd given her. "This is quite good."

"I'm an architect, remember? The best of us are also artists," he responded with total lack of modesty. "Can you help me with this?"

"I'm sure that I can, but if not, one of my jewelers will be able to make something up for you."

David was shaking his head. "That's the last resort. I'm much more interested in your finding an antique pin."

"Well, I'll certainly try. You want it in two weeks?"

"Yes, it's for a very special lady who's leaving town."

Nora glanced up at him, letting him see the look in her eyes this time. David read it easily. "You think this is another farewell gift for another about to be ex-girlfriend?"

"That's not really any of my business, Mr. Sommer," Nora responded, looking away quickly.

"I know, but I'd like to tell you about this lady, about Maggie. She occupies a very special place in my life."

"Really, Mr. Sommer—"

"Maggie has been my secretary for five years," he continued, undaunted. "To tell you the truth, I wooed her away from another architectural firm. She's been my right arm—and my left. Now at the age of sixty-five, she's decided to retire and take off for Peru. That may sound a little crazy, but Maggie loves to travel, and she's always had a yen to see Machu Picchu. She's quite a gal. As a farewell present, I thought she'd like a memento of her trip."

Having expected Maggie to be another Diane, Nora was surprised and secretly a little relieved. "Maggie sounds quite marvelous, and I'm looking forward to the assignment. In two weeks, I guarantee you'll have a llama that will be just right for her."

"I knew I could count on you, Nora. As usual."

Their meeting over, the waiter appeared as if on cue to tell David that his table was ready for lunch. Everything had gone quite well, Nora thought as she slid her chair back. "Thank you for the coffee and for the opportunity. Your request is a delightful one."

"Now I have one more request." When she looked up at him, David thought that he'd never seen such huge, beautiful eyes. "I'd like you to join me for lunch."

Nora's puzzlement lasted only a moment. "That one o'clock luncheon date is for *us*?"

"It is."

"Mr. Sommer, I came to this meeting with the assurance that it wouldn't be a ploy to get me on a date."

"It wasn't. Our appointment was to discuss Maggie's gift. *Now* comes the ploy to entice you to lunch."

"You are incorrigible, Mr. Sommer." But Nora wasn't exasperated. In fact, she was amused by his persistence, and at this point acquiescence seemed easier than argument. David Sommer was a hard man to refuse. "I'd love to have lunch with you," Nora said, and smiled.

David was surprised. He'd expected to have to use all his reserve tactics to win her over. Without even a word of protest, she'd accepted. A broad grin brightened his face.

"I have just one more request, Nora. Please."

She looked up at him questioningly.

"Call me 'David.'"

THEY DECIDED NOT TO GO into the large dining room but to have their lunch at the corner table where they'd been so comfortable. David didn't want to take any chances that her mood would change. It had taken him a long time, many weeks, to reach this stage of their relationship; granted, it wasn't intimate, but at least it was friendly. At this point it was all that he could hope for.

"I come here quite often," he explained to Nora, "and I guarantee the food is excellent."

It was, and during the meal David easily kept the conversation going with questions about Keepsakes. They weren't personal, just interested. He hoped that was apparent to Nora. It seemed to be, for she'd relaxed completely and was obviously enjoying herself.

Over dessert David said, "I'm glad we're talking face to face at last, since our telephone conversations were never that promising."

"I always try to meet with my clients and get to know all about them," Nora admitted.

"Then why have you been avoiding me?"

Nora carefully took a bite of her dessert before answering. "I'm not talking about dates, David." She said his name at last, though a little uncertainly. "I'm talking about getting to know my clients' needs."

"So am I," he said, looking directly at Nora, until she was forced to lower her eyes.

While she was still off guard, David asked, "Why didn't we ever meet early on, two years ago when I first called Keepsakes?"

"You didn't want to."

"What?" He couldn't believe his ears.

"I suggested a meeting at your office or mine, and you declined. Said you didn't have time, that you felt we could communicate quite well over the phone."

"Good Lord," David said, surprised. "What a fool I was. Well, I won't worry about past mistakes but just be glad we finally got together for an enjoyable—" he looked at his watch "—two hours."

"More than two, and I need to be going."

He caught her hand in a grasp that wasn't restraining but still seemed to make her nervous. Quickly he released her. "Don't leave before we make some future plans. I want to see you again, Nora. As often as possible." He was no longer touching her, but his eyes seemed to caress, and so did his voice.

Nora took a deep breath, preparatory to giving him a litany of excuses. "David, today was an exception—"

"I know, professional standards, no dating clients. That went out years ago, as you well know. It's something else. At first I thought that you just didn't like me, but today disproves that. We've had a good time, at least I have." He looked at her steadily, waiting for a response.

"So have I, David," she admitted.

"Then what is it? Is it Diane?"

"I don't know."

"I haven't seen her since that night, haven't even heard from her." David felt the need to explain, make Nora understand that the relationship with Diane wasn't, and never had been, important. "We were going in different directions. Both of us knew that. She enjoyed the parties, the weekends, the big events I sometimes get invited to. In public, we were great. In private, we had nothing to say. Our differences were so obvious."

"Is that what you meant by an 'unrealistic relationship'?"

He seemed surprised. "You remember that?"

"I thought it was a very convenient term at the time, but now I'm beginning to understand."

"Could it be that you've misinterpreted other things about me?"

Again she was evasive. "I don't know." Nora felt she was being drawn into a very personal conversation, something she wasn't sure she wanted.

"Tell me what you think of me," David asked boldly, but this time she wasn't willing, or able, to respond.

"Then I'll tell *you*." He pushed his chair back a little and stretched out his long legs, crossing his arms over his chest. "You think I'm demanding, high-handed and spoiled."

Nora could only smile. He was right on the mark.

"I get what I want," he said, not mincing words. "That's important for me, but isn't it important for everyone?"

"Yes," Nora agreed, "but within certain bounds."

He was thoughtful for a moment, his blue eyes darkening with intensity. "What's really important for me is beauty. Oh, I know that sounds pretentious, but it's true. That's why I want the best gift possible for Maggie. That's why my offices are more attractive than any others in the city. That's why I'm an architect. I want to take hold of all the ugliness in the world and tear it out by the roots."

"You sound like a man with a passion," Nora said softly.

"You'd understand if you'd seen where I grew up, in a sad little town in the middle of nowhere, surrounded by ugliness. Wherever I looked there were mines or quarries or factories. I vowed to get out and get my mother out, too."

"Did you?" she had to ask.

"Yes. My parents live in Florida now, surrounded by flowers and greenery, with no smog to blot out the sun, no repellent odor in the air, no blighted hills or twisted trees. That was my birthright."

"How terrible." Nora thought of her own childhood, surrounded by the beauty of New Orleans.

"It was terrible, but in a way, my salvation. I grew up in an ugly square box of a house with weathered, peeling paint, just like all the other houses in the neighborhood. I really believe that a person can die of ugliness, unremitting, grueling, never-ending ugliness. I was determined not to die there, and that determination got me out. I won a scholarship to Yale and began designing other kinds of buildings that added beauty, not blight, to the landscape."

Nora was very quiet, thinking about the little boy that David had been and the man he'd become.

He saw the look on her face. "This is far too heavy, isn't it? I'm sorry."

"I'm not. I understand you so much better now, particularly since I'd imagined your coming from a wealthy, privileged family, used to giving orders and having every whim catered to."

David nodded. "Sometimes I fit that picture, Nora. Success does that to people. But I worked long and hard to get where I am. It was a tough road, and along the way I had to polish up a lot of rough edges. I even took voice lessons to get rid of the twang so I could fit into the successful world I'd made for myself. I have every intention of enjoying it."

"You're a determined man."

His grin was slow and easy and a bit self-satisfied. "Now perhaps, Nora, you're beginning to understand what I'm all about."

As they left the café, David took her arm and asked, "Can you take the long way home?"

Nora looked puzzled.

"I'd like you to walk over to First Avenue with me. I want to show you the new development I've begun there."

Nora looked down at the antique watch she wore pinned to her lapel. "I've been away from the office for hours," she protested, but only halfheartedly.

"Then another half hour won't matter. I'll admit that there's method to this, another ploy. I'm hoping that when I show you the project, you'll be so impressed with my compassion and imagination that you'll have dinner with me."

"I won't be able to do that, David, because I have plans for tonight, but I'll walk over to First Avenue with you. I'd like to see the culmination of a dream that began so many years ago."

3

AS SHE MOVED from counter to counter in the crowded little gift shop, Nora's frustration began to build. She was having difficulty finding just the right gift for her loyal clients, the duke and duchess. The couple's taste was impeccable, and they shopped constantly for each other, but when it came time to purchase gifts for friends, they were used to depending on Nora. She suspected that they loved the idea of having a personal shopper oceans away; it suited their style, which was definitely noblesse oblige. Nora didn't mind in the slightest, since they spent a small fortune with her and had referred numerous other clients to Keepsakes over the years.

"Don't tell me you're stumped, Nora, dear." The owner of the shop, a tall slim man in his early fifties, approached, a smile on his artificially tanned face. "This may be a first."

"Oh, no, it happens quite frequently, Maurice, but I usually manage to keep my cool. This time is different. I simply don't have an idea in my head."

"Tell Maurice the problem, darling," he said confidentially, "and I'll solve it for you."

There was a sedate jingle of the front bell as another customer entered the shop. Maurice glanced up without interest, nodded for one of his clerks to take over and waited for Nora's explanation.

"The duke and duchess are spending two weeks on their friends' yacht in the Aegean. They need a gift for their hosts."

"Hmm." Maurice rubbed his narrow chin thoughtfully. "They'll be island-hopping, I presume?"

"Oh, I'm sure they'll call in at all those little offbeat Greek and Turkish islands."

"How terribly dull," Maurice decided. "Just imagine their shopping possibilities—sponges and worry beads. That's about it." His laugh was infectious, Nora couldn't help joining in.

"Maybe something to cheer them up after they return from tramping around the ruins," Nora commented.

"Not to mention stuffing themselves on all that rich food. A supply of tablets for indigestion," Maurice teased, "might be in order."

Nora had moved to another corner of the store jammed with objets d'art. None of them appealed to her. She was just about to give up for the day, when Maurice called out. "I know—a game, something to occupy long, dull evenings as they float around in the Aegean. Nora, look, this is it!" Carefully he picked up a chessboard with delicately carved figures. "I just got it in, a unique set, one of a kind. It's a minor miracle."

With relief Nora agreed. "I don't know what I'd ever do without you, Maurice," she said as she glanced at her watch. "Now I'll have time to run home and change for my lunch date."

"I hope he's tall, dark and handsome," Maurice said, handing the chess set to an assistant to pack.

Nora smiled slyly. "He's all that and more, but it's strictly business."

"What a shame."

NORA WAS TYING the wraparound sash of her coolest cotton printed dress, when Janice warned her from the office, "It's almost noon. You're going to be late."

"Then I guess he'll just have to wait," Nora said. She smiled at her reflection in the mirror. For all her complaints about the heat, she'd picked up a little color running around town in the blazing sun. Her slim arms in the short, capped sleeves were golden brown. She slipped on an antique bangle bracelet and nodded with satisfaction at the effect.

"I don't believe what you just said," Janice called out again. "You've never kept David waiting. Sounds as if you're getting awfully sure of yourself—or of him."

Nora applied a touch of gloss to her lips while she thought about that. Then she answered honestly. "I'm not sure of either. I was just joking." She ran a brush through her hair, twisted it expertly into a bun at her nape and turned away from the mirror without another glance. She'd been taking more and more time dressing for her lunch dates with David. Janice was beginning to notice and, as was her habit, to comment.

She did so again when Nora went into the office. "Another spectacular effect," Janice said approvingly, "but it wasn't achieved in what I'd call record time."

"That's because I move slowly in this unseasonably hot weather," Nora explained with a grin. "I've never seen such heat in late September."

Janice wasn't about to be sidetracked. "Well, you look smashing, as you've looked for all your David lunches. They're getting to be a routine, aren't they?"

"Hardly." Nora's denial was quick but not exactly truthful. She and David had met for lunch at least once a week since mid-August, but the rest of her statement was factual. "Every luncheon has been connected with business in some way. First the llama, which was spectacularly successful, and then the anniversary present for his parents."

"The equally successful lithograph, which, I might add, was my idea," Janice said smugly.

Nora continued as if she hadn't been interrupted. "Then there was the incentive gift for the foreman who kept David's East Side project on schedule."

"And finally the birthday present for his draftsman."

Janice managed to keep a straight face as she said, "Each and every gift preceded by a long lunch meeting with the client, namely David Sommer."

"Oh, yes, each and every one," Nora agreed.

"But you really don't enjoy spending all that time with him, right?"

"Not at all," Nora lied without even trying to be convincing. She'd dumped her shoulder bag onto the table and was choosing a few necessary items to stuff into the clutch bag that matched her dress. "Of course I enjoy spending the time with David. He's intelligent, charming and witty." Her voice softened perceptibly, but when she saw the superior look on Janice's face, she added, "but right now he's just a client, one of the very best, I'll admit."

"Why don't you ever go out to dinner with the guy? Live a little, be daring? He's crazy about you."

"That's purely speculation on your part, Janice. David and I are getting to know each other, slowly and surely, and I like it that way."

"David doesn't."

Nora looked up, puzzled.

"Oh, he talks to me all the time, tells me his troubles."

Nora put a compact into her purse, but not without opening it first and adding a touch of powder to her nose. She'd decided not to acknowledge the remark.

Janice watched without comment. Something in her boss's eye must have told her she'd gone far enough. "Well, I'm just glad I didn't take so much time getting to know Dan."

"Janice, you *have* to move fast considering how often you change boyfriends. Besides, Dan owns our messenger service. You've been talking on the phone to him for a couple of years."

Janice smiled at her boss from her cross-legged position on the floor. It was a challenging smile.

"All right, Janice, I know what you're thinking. I've been on the phone with David for years, too, but as for the time we've spent together since we first met, everything is right on schedule."

"On schedule?" Janice rolled her eyes heavenward. "We're not talking about airlines. We're talking about romance."

"*You're* talking about romance," Nora corrected firmly. "I'm talking about friendship. If anything else develops, it'll do so naturally, over time."

"Let nature take its course, right?"

"Exactly." Nora slung the shoulder bag over the back of her desk chair, closed her purse and headed for the door.

Janice's next question stopped her. "Are you concerned about the blonde, Diane?" she asked thoughtfully.

"Not at all. That breakup was final, and very much mutual. Since then David's been spending most of his time concentrating on his work as he finishes up the East Side project." Nora was still lingering at the door, a thoughtful look in her eyes. "It's really special. The first time I saw it I knew he was creating more than just another low-income development."

Nora thought back to the day of their first lunch together, when David had insisted that she take a tour. On the way he told her what he was trying to achieve by renovating those buildings that were salvageable, relics from the past with a beauty of line that should not be forgotten. Because it wasn't possible to capture the same style so many decades later, he'd opted for simplicity in the new structures.

He'd achieved just what he'd hoped for, Nora knew as soon as she'd seen the partially completed project.

"It's charming," she told him. "So warm and—" she searched for the word "—livable."

David grinned. "To tell you the truth, those are just the adjectives I thought of when I first started work. I'm glad it shows."

Nora could see the pride in his blue eyes as he looked around. He loved the project as much as those who would eventually live in it. They walked through the unfinished buildings, and as they walked the workmen called out to David. Everyone seemed to know him; even more surprising, he knew all of them.

"It helps for a planner to be on a first-name basis with the construction team to preserve continuity. Otherwise they're just working from plans on a blueprint or orders from a foreman, and the feeling is lost. I want everyone to like what he's doing as much as I like it. I demand that," he added.

Nora wasn't surprised. David Sommer might have a gut feeling for his work, but he also had an unquenchable ambition, and to be successful, to stay successful, called for tough tactics. Nora imagined that the man who made a mistake in David's employ would not be around long enough to tell about it. She could almost feel his power as she walked around the buildings with him. It was exciting and a little frightening.

"Nora..."

"Yes?" She came out of her reverie at the sound of Janice's voice. "I was just thinking about the East Side project."

"I saw the spread about it in the *Times*."

"That hardly did it justice. I'll ask David to give you a tour now that it's almost complete. He's combined low-income housing with commercial property so the low rents can offset the high ones, and somehow he's managed to keep the personality of the neighborhood."

Nora caught herself, realizing that she was expounding the virtues of a man she claimed was only a client, certainly no more than a friend. "It's time to go," she said quickly, "or I really will be late."

"Sure, boss. See you later." The phone was ringing as Nora left. She hadn't even reached the elevator when Janice caught up with her.

"I think you ought to take this call."

"Who is it?"

"I don't know—that's what's so weird." Janice tried to explain as Nora followed her back to the office. "He wouldn't give his name, and I'm sure he's not a client, but he sounds like he knows you really well. He says its urgent."

DAVID LOOKED IMPATIENTLY toward the door of the restaurant, then at his watch, then back at the door. Nora was fifteen minutes late for their lunch date, which worried David, because she'd been so punctual in the past. He considered calling her office and then thought better of it. His anxiety was getting out of hand, but at least he could keep it from showing.

"Would you care to order a drink, Mr. Sommer?" Obviously it *was* showing. The waiter had noticed.

David shook his head. "I'll wait." This was just another example of his confusion about Nora. He wondered for the thousandth time where things were going with her. Then he smiled cynically. He knew where they were going. Nowhere.

Sure, they'd spent time together, long lunches at Darcy's, friendly hours with lots of talk. They'd discussed their respective business, their travels, their likes and dislikes. She drank iced coffee by the gallon and hated Mexican food; she was allergic to cats and didn't know how to ski. She read detective stories and listened to Bach. He knew all that, but he still didn't know her, the nuances of Nora, how she felt and what she thought. He didn't understand her wants, her needs. Each time he tried to get close enough to find the real Nora, she put up a screen.

David was still brooding over their relationship, when he looked up and saw Nora coming toward him. Her face was flushed, there were patches of pink in her cheeks and her eyes seemed especially bright. He'd never seen her look so beautiful. David stood up and reached for her hand. He wanted to kiss one of her cheeks, feel her soft skin against his face, but he'd never done more than take her hand in greeting or put his arm around her waist as he helped seat her or as they walked along together after their lunches. So once more he settled for the touch of her hand.

"Sorry I'm late," Nora said as she dropped into the chair. David smiled and was about to tell her no apology was necessary; he was just glad she was here. Then he noticed that the flush on her face represented neither heat nor hurry. She was upset. He'd seen her amused, occasionally even irritated. He'd never seen her visibly upset.

He ordered two glasses of wine before asking in a voice that he kept casual, "Did you get caught in the traffic?"

"No. I got caught in something at the office." The wine came, and she took not a sip but a gulp as David watched, his eyes narrowed.

"Problems?"

"Not really." Her smile was tremulous, and her eyes were still bright, even though the wine was beginning to relax her a little. "It's not important."

"I think it is, Nora. You don't seem yourself at all."

David thought the silence that followed was never going to end. He was about to prod her again, when he saw the tears building in her eyes. Without a word, he reached across the table and took her hand. The gesture wasn't planned, as his greetings always were, it was spontaneous.

"Tell me about it, Nora." She still didn't speak. "I'm here for you, and I want to help if I can."

The tears that welled up didn't spill down her cheeks, but David knew she was forcibly holding them back, and that caused him pain. Whatever was upsetting Nora, it was no simple problem associated with work. "This isn't Keepsakes, is it?" He hoped he could lead her into explaining.

She shook her head and then said quietly, "No. But it's nothing earthshaking, either. I feel like such a fool getting upset." After taking a deep breath, she explained, "I just got a phone call from my father." Once more the tremor came into her voice, and she took another sip of wine, a small one this time, just to soothe her dry throat.

"I've never heard you mention your father."

"No, I don't talk about him."

"I knew your mother died years ago, so I just assumed he wasn't alive, either."

"Oh, he's very much alive." There was more than sarcasm in her voice, there was bitterness, too. David sat quietly, waiting. Now that she'd mentioned her father, the ice was broken and she could talk about him, but not until she was ready. David was willing to be patient.

"His name is Phillip Chase," Nora said finally in a voice that was strong and even. "And I haven't seen him in almost fifteen years."

"Why, Nora?"

"Whatever the reasons, they were of his own choosing."

"What happened?" David couldn't stop the questions coming now. He wanted to know everything.

"David, could I have another glass of wine? I think I'm going to need it." Nora laughed almost sadly.

"Not on an empty stomach. Especially when you're a woman who sips at one glass for hours and still leaves it half-full." He gestured to the waiter, ordered pasta salads for both of them and two more glasses of white wine. Only when the meal arrived and after another sip of wine did Nora explain.

"Phillip walked out on my mother and me fifteen years ago, and I haven't seen him since. Oh, I've received an occasional postcard or letter, even a gift now and then, but nothing—not a word—in the past few years. Now he's in New York, and he wants to see me."

David released Nora's hand so that she could eat lunch, but noticed that she didn't pick up her fork. "Do you want to see him?"

"No, I don't. I've gotten along fine without Phillip all these years. I have no desire to let him back into my life."

"So you said no?"

"I tried to, but he was determined, insistent, really. There wasn't much I could do. He's coming over tonight." After a pause Nora added, "And to tell the truth, part of me is just the slightest bit curious."

"I don't blame you. Fifteen years is a long time. So much has changed. You're a grown woman, and he's probably past middle age."

"He's sixty. His birthday was June 12," she added matter-of-factly.

"He has a lot of time to make up."

"He can never make it up," Nora said calmly.

"You sound pretty sure of that."

"I am. Some things we lose can never be replaced."

"Sounds like you didn't get along with Phillip." But even as David spoke he couldn't help thinking that she'd remembered her father's birthday after all these years.

"I got along with him very well," Nora said. "In fact, I adored him. That's what makes it so difficult." David began to understand.

"My father was a gambler," Nora explained. "Not the kind who took trips to Las Vegas or hung around race-tracks, although he's been known to do that, too. He was more interested in get-rich-quick schemes. The greater the risk, the higher the stakes, the better his chance of making a fortune. Except he rarely did. By the time I was born he'd gone through most of his inheritance, and he spent my childhood years trying to recoup."

"That must have been a shaky existence." David could see the pain of remembering—and maybe some of the pleasure—in Nora's eyes.

"When I was younger I thought it was fun, a wonderful game. Sometimes we'd be rich, or what I considered rich, and go to Antoine's for lunch. The waiters would hover over us, and my father would tip extravagantly. On the way home he'd buy me gifts—toys, dolls—anything I wanted. The next week, he'd have to sell off the antique bedroom furniture or my grandmother's silver. He'd always promise Mother that he'd get it back."

"But he never did."

"No, he never did." Nora had begun to nibble at her salad, and it occurred to David that those bittersweet memories were good for her in a way. At least talking about them seemed to help.

"We used to have marvelous parties. I remember one in particular. I was too young to attend, but I watched from the top of the stairs while waiters served champagne and caviar and the orchestra played. Mother was in her room crying, wondering how we'd pay for it all, but Phillip had a deal going, and he needed to impress people."

"That kind of life couldn't have been easy for your mother."

"It wasn't. Of course, both of them being from respectable New Orleans families, divorce was considered unseemly."

"Yet they finally did break up?"

"Yes. When I was about sixteen. Mother just couldn't take it anymore, and I think he knew the time had come for him to leave. I've always thought they loved each other, but it was an impossible situation. Frankly, I would never have been as long-suffering as my mother."

Nora paused for a moment, and David urged her to finish her lunch.

"I think I will," she said with a smile. "I'm feeling much better. Thank you, David."

"For what?"

"For listening."

"I want to know everything about you," he said truthfully. "What happened after he left, when you were sixteen?" He thought to himself what a lovely sixteen-year-old she must have been, with long brown hair and those dark, dark eyes and golden skin. She'd never avoided the sun. Even now there was a slight trace of freckles across her nose that had probably been more noticeable at sixteen, but the real beauty had come later, with maturity. He was sure that at that moment she was more beautiful than she'd ever been.

"The year before he left we moved out of the big house. The bank took it, I guess. We rented a smaller house in an awful part of New Orleans. I hated it. I didn't even want my friends to visit us because I was so ashamed. That was really no problem, though, because I left them all behind when I changed schools. I'd always been to private school until then. Lord knows how my father paid for it, if in fact he did pay."

Nora must have sensed what the look in David's eyes meant, because she quickly added, "Don't feel sorry for me. I'm not telling you this for sympathy. Lots of people have had a harder life than mine. My mother and father both loved me. They had different ways of showing it, that's all. Mother was a little distant but very protective. Phillip was warm and loving. Of course, he was also totally irresponsible."

"I'm not feeling sorry for you, Nora," David said. "It's less sympathy than surprise that I feel. Looking at you now, I can hardly imagine that your family was ever bereft."

Nora laughed. "Despite my father's penchant for gambles that didn't pay off, he managed to give me one permanent gift, and that was good taste. It's certainly served me well in my business."

"You didn't inherit your sense of responsibility, however," David said with a smile.

"In a way I did," Nora countered, "by compensating for his lack with a double supply myself. I was determined to make my way in the world and never be poor again. That determination put me through business school. One semester I held down three different jobs."

David shook his head in amazement. "Quite a gal," he said as much to himself as to Nora.

"Quite a talkative one, anyway. I didn't mean to bore you to death over lunch."

"Don't prejudge me, Nora. You've done that before. I wasn't bored in the slightest. I'm glad you told me about your family, because it helps me to understand." David could see that the attention was making Nora a little self-conscious. She was ready to talk about something else or maybe even to leave. He wasn't going to let her, though, not yet. "When did your mother die?"

"While I was in business school. She'd had a strange life, difficult in many ways, but surprisingly enough, she wasn't any happier when my father left. Somehow I think she really enjoyed that up-and-down life of ours."

David didn't say anything. He wasn't a doctor and had no intention of psychoanalyzing Nora's parents, but because of what he now knew about them, he was able to understand them better. She'd had a difficult childhood with a father she loved, who left her at an impressionable age. Now Phillip Chase was returning. No wonder she was upset, and no wonder, he thought, not for the first time today, she was so wary of men and so damned independent.

"Would you like me to be there with you tonight? I don't have any plans." He knew the answer, but he had to ask.

"No, I'll be fine. I'm sure Phillip won't stay long. What can we say to each other after almost fifteen years?" She forced a brittle smile.

"Maybe a great deal," he ventured.

"I doubt it. There's really no way to catch up on all that lost time, and even if there were, I have no desire to." She was ready to go now, David could tell. She'd shared all she intended to, and the door to her feelings was closing. "I need to be getting back," she said simply.

David walked with her to the street and hailed a cab. There was just the slightest hint of a cool breeze, the first indication that fall was on its way. Somehow that seemed to brighten Nora's spirits, and maybe it was just that nip in the air that caused David to lean over and kiss her on the cheek. It was a gesture that seemed so right, and to the gesture he added his thanks for what she'd just shared with him. "I'm glad I had this opportunity to hear about your father. Just remember that I'll be home tonight, and I'll be thinking about you. Call if you need me, Nora."

There was a look of gratitude in her eyes, a look that meant much more to him than Nora could know.

"Thanks," she said. "I'll remember." With that she turned and got into the cab, but David remained standing on the curb, his mind full of her.

NORA THOUGHT OF changing her clothes, putting on something a little more casual, then decided against it. This wasn't to be a casual, fun evening. There'd be no letting her hair down, sitting around in jeans and chatting with her dear old dad. Their meeting would no doubt be stiff and formal; that was fine with Nora.

She settled down at her desk for a few minutes, looking over the mail and signing the letters Janice had left for her, busying herself with work until it was time for Phillip to arrive. Then she closed up the office and went into the more formal living room, turning on a table lamp near the door.

Nora had never liked overhead light in a room; in fact, she'd had all the ceiling lights in her apartment removed in favor of softer lamplight, and she knew why. To Phillip Chase, lighting had always been a fundamental part of the decorating scheme. That wasn't all that the daughter had inherited from her father. Looking around the formal living room, Nora realized that every piece of furniture, carefully collected over the years as she'd been able to afford them, reflected her background. Phillip would like the room, and for a brief moment she almost wished it were done in a modern black-and-white style that would disprove a connection between them.

The phone rang, surprising Nora, who'd been expecting to hear the doorbell. She answered with the hope that it would be her father canceling their meeting. That would certainly have been typical, a call saying something had come up and he'd have to see her later. Later, to Phillip Chase, could be a matter of hours or years.

But the caller wasn't her father, it was David. "I know it's time for him to be there," David said apologetically, "but I just had to hear your voice and be sure you were all right. Besides, something tells me your father is the type who doesn't keep to a schedule."

Nora laughed. Hearing David's voice was just what she needed. "You're absolutely right about that. I can't remember that he was ever on time."

"Are you ready for him?"

"I think so. I was just standing here looking around my living room and being reminded of the similarity in our tastes—and wishing it weren't so."

It was David's turn to laugh. "Don't tell me you'd rather have bad taste than be compared to your father."

"Maybe we both have bad taste. Who knows?"

"I know," David said quickly, "without ever having seen your apartment. I know it's lovely, just as you're lovely. Of course, I can never be absolutely certain until you invite me to dinner."

"Soon," Nora found herself saying.

"Is that a promise?"

"It's a promise. I'm not much of a cook, though, I must tell you."

"That's all right, I'll bring something. Do you like Chinese?"

"I love it." To Nora's relief, the conversation had drifted away from her father to her and David. She knew that's what David had intended, and she was thankful to him.

They talked until the downstairs buzzer rang. David could hear it on his end of the line, and so he left her with more easy patter. "Don't worry about not being able to recognize him after all these years. He'll be the one standing in the hall when you open the door."

Nora was still laughing at that as she buzzed her father in through the downstairs security system and then waited for him to take the elevator to her floor. She didn't need to reflect on how he would look or even how he'd act. She knew he'd still be handsome and he'd still be charming. The years couldn't have changed those aspects, at least. Her thoughts were more negative. Maybe she owed him the courtesy of this visit, but she owed him little else. Yet if he asked for money, she supposed she'd give it to him. Then he'd leave and everything would be back to normal.

When the front doorbell chimed, Nora took a deep breath, willed her hands to stop shaking, set a smile in place and walked into the foyer.

The bell chimed again. Slowly she opened the door.

"Hello, there, beautiful. Don't you have a kiss for your old dad?"

HER MEMORIES and the more tangible photographs were all she'd had of her father for fifteen years. Nora expected to see certain changes in him, but she was surprised to find him much like the man she remembered.

There were lines on his face that certainly hadn't been there before, deep creases along the sides of his mouth, furrows between his brows and crinkly crow's-feet around his eyes that intensified when he smiled, as he was doing now, broadly. His hair, which had once been jet black, was flecked with gray but still thick and wavy, combed back from his forehead and worn long on the sides, just as she remembered.

Nora saw all this in the few seconds while he stood motionless before her. Then he took a step forward and swept her into his arms, as he'd done so often until she was sixteen years old and he'd walked out of her life. He must have felt her body stiffen, for he released her quickly, yet not without a kiss on the cheek.

"How's my girl?" he asked, taking her arm and walking beside her down the hall to the living room.

"I'm fine, Phillip," she answered, hardly paying attention to her response or to the polite inquiry that followed. "How are you?"

He smiled in answer, and Nora realized he'd caught on. Her greeting had been cool and so had her first words. There wasn't going to be a big, wonderful reunion. He had no right to expect that, and yet he kept his smile, didn't release her arm.

She finally extracted herself from his hold and crossed the room to the antique ice chest that she used as a bar. "Would you like something to drink?" she asked, turning back to him.

"You're beautiful, Nora," he said, ignoring her offer. "So much like your mother."

Nora fought to keep the tightness from her voice. "People in New Orleans say I look like you."

"The coloring, maybe, but not the rest. The shape of your face, that slightly upward slant of your eyes, *everything* about your mouth. All pure Margaret." He was looking at her with such deep scrutiny, as if trying to memorize her, that it made Nora nervous, especially since the features he mentioned *were* like her mother's. Nora couldn't help glancing at the large photograph on a table near the doorway where Phillip was still standing.

Phillip saw her eyes travel to it and reached down to pick up the gilt-framed picture. "Oh, yes, I remember this one," he said in a voice that almost tugged at Nora's heart.

Almost, but not quite. She caught herself before she fell under his spell. Her father had always been able to get a little catch in his voice, bring a random tear to his eye at will. "Something to drink?" she repeated.

"A martini would be fine."

"Sorry," she said almost gladly. "I don't have any vermouth."

"Then just pour some gin over ice for your old daddy," he said in a voice that came straight out of the Old South. He could use his accent very effectively or drop it entirely, depending on the circumstances and his listeners. Today he was trying it on for nostalgia, Nora supposed.

It didn't work. She fixed his drink, handed it to him and then offered him a seat, but he remained standing, one hand in his pocket, the other holding his drink. Nora was feeling very uptight, and her father's easy manner just made her feel worse, until she saw the telltale twitch of a muscle in his cheek and knew he wasn't quite as cool as he seemed. But he was certainly as observant as ever.

"I like the Biedermeier chairs against that wall. Very effective."

"Thank you." Nora poured herself a glass of white wine and sat down on the sofa. Phillip joined her. Politely he'd waited for her to be seated. He'd always been a gentleman, that hadn't changed.

On the other hand, he'd never minced his words, so his next remark didn't surprise Nora. "The chairs must have cost a fortune."

"I've been collecting slowly over the years. Those are the most recent pieces." Nora was beginning to be annoyed by this pointless talk. However, she certainly didn't want it to become any more familiar, any more real, so she remained silent and waited for another observation from Phillip.

"You must have done well with your business." When she nodded, he said, "I like the name. Keepsakes," he mused.

For some reason, hearing him say the word made her angry. She suddenly thought of all the keepsakes of the past that had been taken from her, of the bare house she and her mother had been left in, of the years it had taken just to buy these few things to furnish her apartment. She'd bought most of them at auction, keepsakes from other people whose lives had gone the way of Phillip Chase's. Nora clutched her wineglass so tightly she was afraid the stem might break. Trying to relax, she said, "I've worked hard and I've been lucky."

"Luck has nothing to do with your choice of furniture. That's called taste," Phillip observed.

"I owe that to you," Nora had to admit.

Phillip made a little gesture of salute with his glass before he took another swallow. "I've always loved fine antiques. Even those that I was only able to keep for a short time," he added, and Nora realized this was as close as he was going to come to admitting what had happened to him—to all of them—in the past. "That's why I've enjoyed living abroad for the past few years."

For the first time Nora realized that Phillip hadn't even been in the same country as his daughter. "Where did you live?"

"Rome. Florence. Paris. All breathtaking cities. Do you know Florence? It's my favorite, I believe."

Nora shook her head and tried to control the little spark of anger that insinuated itself into her voice as she responded flatly, "I've never traveled abroad."

Impervious, Phillip continued, "I remember a lovely little pension in Florence, inexpensive but perfect. What one needs in order to travel is a sense of adventure and perhaps the ability to take risks."

That last remark really made Nora angry, and she no longer tried to control the feeling. He'd forgotten all about the risks that had ended in failure and suffering for his family. To her anger was added a bitterness that was perfectly justified, Nora realized. This was the man who, with his charm and wit and good taste, had tried to con the world and ultimately failed, the man who'd never done an honest day's work in his life. And this man had the audacity to suggest that it would be a simple matter to go traveling around Europe.

Nora got up abruptly and moved to the other side of the room. "I have too many responsibilities here to take time out for travel," she said, purposely implying that he had no such problem.

Phillip managed, quite easily she thought, to ignore the implication. Nora watched him sitting there on the sofa, his arm along the back, his long legs stretched out, comfortably, as if he owned the place. His three-piece suit, which was made of a rough-textured silk, beige with flecks of brown woven through it, was just his style. She wondered who'd bought it for him. Something told her he didn't have the money to pay for such expensive clothes himself, otherwise he wouldn't be here in her living room. That he was here for financial reasons, Nora had no doubt.

Yet she could be wrong. She didn't know the answer to anything at this point, nor did she understand her feelings for Phillip. So many different emotions were warring in her that she had no idea which one would emerge next. She both loved him and hated him, felt sorry for him and was disgusted with him, admired his good looks, his savoir faire, his charm—and despised the use he put them to.

On the verge of expressing her anger, Nora was suddenly ashamed of it. There was no question that the man had confused her totally, and all the while he sat there, calm, collected, the same old Phillip. For one brief moment he'd almost admitted how he'd squandered away all the beautiful things that should have belonged to the next generations of his family. But he'd caught himself quickly, and it wouldn't happen again, she'd bet. Conversely, Nora had no idea what she would do or say next. She remained a bundle of nerves waiting for the next reaction.

Phillip didn't make it easy for her. "I want to know everything about you, Nora, everything that's happened since I saw you last."

"That would be difficult," she said coolly. "It's been fifteen years."

"Fifteen years," he repeated with a kind of wonder in his voice. "That's hard to believe."

Nora wanted to reply that it was very easy for her to believe. She remembered every year, especially those early ones when she'd been only a teenage girl, waiting for him, wondering when he'd return. But she held back her antagonism. That made her even more nervous. She was beginning to doubt that she'd ever get through this meeting. She took a deep breath and sat down on the love seat across the room from her father.

"How about if I ask you some specific questions? You can bring me up to date that way." Without waiting for a response, he cleared up a little of the background himself. "I know you graduated with honors from college. I sent you a gift, didn't I?"

"I believe so." She knew very well that he had. He'd sent a pair of gold earrings. She still wore them.

"After college you moved to New York?"

"Yes, I worked for several years in retail."

"Then you started your own business. That's very risky."

"I did a great deal of research, and of course I had a long list of clients whom I knew would patronize such a business." She didn't want to think of herself as taking risks, even though that's exactly what she'd done.

"You've never married?" he asked bluntly. But it was more a statement than a question.

"No, I haven't."

"Is there anyone important in your life?"

The image of David came vividly, poignantly to her mind and then was gone. "No," she said, "there's no one."

"That's too bad," Phillip mused. "Some man out there is missing quite a woman."

The words were gently said, and Nora felt her eyes welling up with tears. How dared he come back after so many years and pry into all the lonely recesses of her life?

Phillip extracted a cigar from the inside breast pocket of his suit. "Do you mind if I smoke?" he asked.

"There's an ashtray on the end table," Nora answered. She'd forgotten that her father had always been a cigar smoker. He'd also done his share of heavy drinking, and yet here he was at sixty looking as fit as ever. Nothing seemed to take its toll on Phillip Chase.

"I didn't marry again," he said, answering a question she hadn't asked. "After your mother there was never anyone important in my life. Oh, there've been women, Lord knows, but no one—"

"Phillip," Nora interrupted, unable to control herself any longer, "what are you doing here?"

"I've come to see you, Nora."

"But why, *why*?"

"To find out how my girl is doing after all this time. Fifteen years, you tell me, although I can't believe—"

"Phillip, what do you want? Is it money? Have you come to ask me for money?"

He didn't answer immediately but sat looking at her with a hurt expression in his dark brown eyes. He hasn't lost his touch, Nora thought, expecting that his voice would quaver a little when he responded.

Not only did he react with his voice, his words were suitably pitiful. "I deserve that," he said, pausing for effect. "Naturally you'd think I was after something."

She ignored his act. "Aren't you?" she demanded.

"Yes, I am. In a way."

He wasn't going to get out of this by playing on her sympathy. "Then tell me, Phillip. Let's stop these games."

Phillip stood up and crossed the room to Nora. He stopped in front of her and reached down to touch her cheek. She didn't pull away.

"I want my daughter back," he said simply. "I know that seems strange after so long, but I guess it's just taken me a while to grow up. All those years ago, when your mother and I separated, I thought about you often."

"I was only a teenager. You could have kept in touch with me." Nora felt her own voice breaking. It wasn't an act, and she suddenly wondered if Phillip's feelings were just as sincere.

He sat down beside her on the love seat. "I did write for a long time, letters to your mother for her to share with you."

"She never showed them to me," Nora said blankly.

"And I never received any answers. I'm sure she thought you were better off without me. Pretty soon I convinced myself that I was better off, too, better off alone. She was wrong, and so was I. Is it a sin to be wrong?"

Nora didn't answer. They were no longer responding directly to each other but to their own confused emotions, for she was convinced now that Phillip was as confused as she.

"So much time has passed." Nora was almost pleading now. "How can we ever be close again?"

"I don't know," he said. "But we have to try—*I* have to try, Nora. Because if I don't I'll lose my last chance."

Nora glanced sharply at him, surprised at the ring of finality in his voice. "Last chance—isn't that rather dramatic?" She held her breath, waiting for him to laugh or to shrug off her question with a smart answer. Yet somehow she knew that wouldn't happen.

"I look tanned and fit, they tell me, much younger than my actual years."

"Yes, you do," Nora agreed, afraid of what was coming.

"The fact is . . . I don't know how to say this except to tell the truth, Nora. I've come back to you because I don't have much longer."

"Phillip . . ."

"I . . . I'm dying, Nora, and I have nowhere else to go."

THE NEXT THING NORA REMEMBERED clearly was walking along Central Park West. With darkness, it had grown much cooler, and there was a real feeling of fall in the air. She'd put on jeans and a sweater. Her hair was still pulled back in a bun at her nape, and she could feel the wind nipping at her ears. Striding along in the early evening as the season began to change, Nora tried to concentrate on that, concentrate on the weather and her sensations.

It didn't work. She found herself thinking about nothing but Phillip.

He'd left less than half an hour earlier, and the minute the door closed behind him Nora had changed clothes, stuffed her keys in her pocket and begun to walk. She wanted to be alone, she told herself, to have time to think.

Yet for the first few blocks she stubbornly avoided all thoughts of him. When she finally opened herself to them, she faced a jumble of feelings, half formed and less than a fraction understood.

It was like an awful nightmare, except it was real. Phillip was real—he was back in her life. The emotional roller coaster ride was just beginning.

Nora turned the corner and stopped in front of a brownstone. She had thought her walk was aimless, wandering. She'd been wrong. It had brought her right to David's. She pushed through the glass door and strode across the lobby to the elevator. The doors slid open, and two couples emerged, laughing and talking. Nora stepped in and pressed the button for his floor.

Only when she found herself standing in front of David's door did she hesitate. She'd only been to his apartment once before, the evening she'd arrived too late with the music box. This time she had arrived unannounced. His plans could have changed; he could have someone with him. She shouldn't have come, or at the very least should have called first. Despite those thoughts, Nora didn't turn away. She rang the bell. She needed someone to talk to, and not just anyone. She needed David Sommer.

He was there before the second ring. Like her, David was dressed in jeans and a sweater, but he was barefoot. "Nora," he said, relief in his voice. "I just called your apartment. When there was no answer, I began to worry. Please, come in."

Nora let herself be led into the apartment. It looked wonderfully inviting. In fact, David looked that way, too, an expression of deep interest, even concern for her, in his eyes.

He settled her on the comfortable, overstuffed sofa and sat down beside her. "I guess I should put on my shoes, but I don't want to take the time. Tell me about it. Obviously you saw him."

"Oh, yes, I saw him."

He read the look in her eyes. "Pretty rough, huh?"

"Much worse than I'd ever imagined. I'd expected that we'd have a drink and talk a little about ourselves without delving into any deep feelings. He'd probably have a second drink, and then I'd give him money and he'd go away. That was the scenario I'd worked out."

"It didn't happen like that?"

"We talked, but it was so personal, David. Not like I'd planned at all." Tears glimmered in her eyes, and David reached out to take her hand. "He talked about Mother, and he asked about me, whether I was happy and in love. Oh, David, I wanted to hate him. Part of me did hate him, but another part . . ." She couldn't explain.

"So you found yourself getting to like the old guy," David said softly.

"No." She was adamant. "I don't like him at all, but I feel connected to him."

"That's understandable, Nora. He is your father, no matter what. The meeting was bound to be difficult, but it's all over now." Still holding her hand, David put his other arm around her shoulders, and Nora let herself relax, leaning her head against his chest.

"I thought it would be over, but it's not. I tried to tell myself I was going to send him on his way."

"But you didn't?"

Nora shook her head. "I can't. Not now, David. I can't."

David looked down at her. "You're reconciled so quickly? That doesn't sound like Nora Chase. I never thought of you as the kind of woman who makes quick and easy emotional decisions."

"I'm not." Nora slipped away from David, got up and walked over to the wide floor-to-ceiling window. The lights of the city flickered before her, but she saw nothing. Standing in front of the panoramic view, she wrapped her arms around her as if she needed some kind of support from the outside in order to speak her next words.

"He's dying, David."

"What?" David remained on the sofa, looking up at her stricken, pale face, too stunned at first to move.

For a moment Nora could do nothing but nod. Then she ran her tongue across dry lips and said, "He has a terminal disease, an inoperable tumor. He's seen the best doctors in France. He's even been treated at a clinic in Switzerland. The radiation did shrink the tumor and bought him a little more time, but the outcome hasn't changed. The prognosis is still the same." Nora looked out the window again, still seeing nothing. "Now he's come home to die. Except that he has no home."

David moved then, surging upward from the sofa and crossing toward her in one fluid motion, taking her in his arms. Nora was much more fragile than he'd imagined in his fantasies. Her ribs felt delicate, almost breakable, beneath his touch. He tried to hold her gently.

"Poor Nora," he said. "To find your father and then to lose him. I'm so sorry."

"He wants to come and live with me, stay at least for a while...."

"Phillip Chase is not without nerve, is he?" David mused. "To descend on a daughter he hasn't seen in years, a child he abandoned, and ask for help. That's damned impertinent." David couldn't control his anger at what this man who hardly knew Nora was doing to her.

"He has nowhere else to go, David. That's what I'm faced with, or part of it. There's more...." She moved away from him, and he let her go. Hoping that she would finish her thoughts, he didn't reach for her again or follow. But she was still silent.

Finally David asked, "Are you going to take him in?" He knew the answer, but she continued to avoid it.

"I could give him money and rent a room for him somewhere. He doesn't have to live with me." Nora spoke the words very firmly, as if convincing herself.

"No, he doesn't," David agreed, waiting for Nora to complete her earlier thought.

"But there's the rest of it."

"Yes," he said, already understanding.

"If I turn him away now, I lose my last chance to know my father. If he dies—when he dies—that opportunity will be gone forever."

"And if you turn him away, you'll regret it all your life."

Nora smiled. "I may regret *not* turning him away. I told him he could move in tomorrow. Oh, Lord, David, I hope I've done the right thing."

She wanted to laugh and cry at the same time, it was all so bizarre, but instead Nora walked toward David and right into his arms, finding the comfort she needed there.

For David it was more important than before, because she'd come to him. He cradled her close. "What can I do to help, Nora?"

"Just be here for me. I need a friend very much."

"I'll always be here." David was filled with mixed emotions. His concern for her was strong and deeply-felt, but it warred with the desire that was building inside him.

The paleness was gone from Nora's face, her cheeks were flushed. There were tears on her thick lashes, and as he watched, one fell onto her cheekbone. He wanted to kiss the tear away, to hold her and kiss her until all the sadness and confusion disappeared.

His arms tightened around her. It was then that Nora looked up at him, awareness growing in her dark eyes. He was sure that she would pull away again, but she didn't. Instead her arms slid around his neck. He felt her breasts against him, felt their warmth; in fact, he felt her soft, enticing warmth all along the length of his body.

"Nora." He breathed her name as he bent toward her. Gently his tongue touched the teardrop on her cheek. It was salty and sweet at the same time. Her face was tilted toward him, and her eyes were closed, the eyelashes dark and sooty against the smoothness of her cheeks.

David looked down at her for a long, sweet moment before his mouth found hers, tentatively at first and then more surely as her lips opened beneath his. He explored the silken recesses of her mouth until he felt her tongue touching his, almost shyly but with an incredibly sensuous provocativeness.

He could hardly believe that she was his at last, no longer a fantasy but a wonderful reality. How he'd wanted her since that night when she'd walked into his apartment weeks ago, cool and efficient and incredibly beautiful. Now her coolness had turned to warmth, her efficiency to vulnerability. He'd never hoped to find her here, like this, in his arms.

Because he'd begun the kiss a little uncertainly and because she'd responded similarly, the passion that followed was almost more than David could handle. His desire was a pounding pulse inside his brain. He could feel the blood drumming through every vein in his body. He wanted her as he'd never wanted anyone before and, miraculously, he felt her response and knew that it duplicated his own.

And it did, for Nora was caught up in their passion. She felt as if she were swirling through a deep, endless pool of unfamiliar and tantalizing sensations. David's mouth on hers, strong and sweet, his warm hands around her waist, his hard body pressing against hers— all this she experienced with near astonishment, with wonder that she could respond so fully.

For a brief moment, when his lips first touched hers, she'd thought of pulling away from him, telling him that she wasn't ready yet, but she couldn't because she *was* ready. She wanted his kiss, his arms around her. She needed them more than she'd ever needed anything in her life.

With rising passion, Nora tightened her arms around his neck. One hand curved into the crisp texture of his hair, the other clung to the hard muscles of his shoulder. As his tongue touched hers, she felt herself responding, pressing closer, melting into him. She kissed him as fervently as he kissed her, and deep, deep inside she began to melt, to let go. The feeling was exhilarating, frightening, exciting all at the same time. She gave herself to it as she gave herself to him. There was no turning back.

Yet she had to turn back. As much as she wanted to lie in David's arms and know him completely, totally, to feel his body, hard and strong, naked beside her, she knew it would be wrong. Not for always but at least for tonight, because she would be using David. Tonight he was her refuge from her father, from the turmoil that was raging inside her. To turn to him in lovemaking at such a time would be unfair to David, it would also be wrong for her.

Nora relaxed her almost desperate hold, dropping her hands from his shoulders and ending their long kiss. She could hear his heart pounding, she could hear the ragged rhythm of his breath, but as she listened, his heartbeat slowed and his breathing relaxed. He held her patiently, quietly, as if he knew her decision.

Without mentioning what had happened between them, Nora looked up at him and said, "I think it's time for me to go."

"Yes." He smiled and touched her cheek, and the touch was sweet but without the passion of moments before. "I know how you're feeling," he said. "This is all mixed up with your father. But something good is also happening, something between us. Let's don't forget that, Nora."

"I won't forget," she said softly.

"Good." He touched her cheek again. "Now I'm going to walk you home." They were still looking deeply into each other's eyes, sharing feelings unspoken. "I guess I'd better put on some shoes first."

They both laughed, almost with relief. David disappeared into the bedroom, came back wearing an old pair of topsiders and grabbed her hand. He pulled her along to the door with a playfulness that made Nora laugh again and relax.

With David still holding her hand, they left the apartment, walked to the corner and turned up Columbus Avenue. "Well, back in the madding crowd," he said. "That's one thing you can always depend on. The Upper West Side never sleeps."

"And never stops eating dinner," Nora added.

"True," David said. They passed one trendy little restaurant after another, all jammed with diners at eleven o'clock in the evening. "But why they insist on eating at outside tables in this changeable weather is more than I can understand. Maybe the wine warms them up," he observed as they passed a table full of rowdy diners lifting their glasses in what was obviously not their first toast. "It certainly can't be the food," he added. "The six or seven bites of nouvelle cuisine that make up a meal could hardly warm a person's cockles."

David was doing his best to lift Nora's spirits, and he was succeeding admirably. Glad to see her laughing, he made his comments sillier and sillier, and pretty soon she joined in. They found something to say about everyone they passed, not just the adults, but the children asleep in carriages instead of at home in bed, where they belonged, or the dogs straining at leashes as they got pulled along on unwanted late-night walks.

By the time they reached Nora's block, David had put his arm around her shoulder and drawn her close. In the window of a high-rise building, he caught their reflection and smiled to himself. They looked just like any other couple out enjoying themselves in the neighborhood. David liked that; it felt good.

Outside the door to Nora's apartment building, two young boys were selling roses. "They probably stole them from the corner florist," David said sotto voce.

Nora laughed but disagreed. "I know those boys. Their father actually grows roses in his tiny backyard over by the river. These must be the last ones of the summer."

"The last *one* of the summer, to be more precise," David remarked. Another couple had just bought a big bunch, leaving one forlorn rose in the tattered green wrapping. "Wonder why they didn't take it?"

"Wrong shade of red, the guy told me," one of the boys answered.

"Well, I think it's the perfect shade of red," David said, pulling a couple of bills from his pocket. "Perfect for my girl." With a flourish, he handed the flower to Nora.

Then the laughter stopped. The boys had taken their money—much more than they'd expected—and headed for the subway, leaving Nora and David standing alone on a sidewalk that was suddenly empty and quiet.

"It's a beautiful rose," Nora said, "and it smells wonderful."

David stood silently watching her. The streetlight reflected on her dark hair and gleamed along the line of her high cheekbone. The petals of the rose brushed against her face. It was a beautiful flower, but it was nothing compared to the woman who held it. "I should buy you dozens of roses," he said. "Fill your apartment with them."

"That wouldn't mean any more than this one. It's special."

David agreed. "It's a special night," he answered quietly.

"And you're a special friend."

David linked her arm in his, and together they went through the doors into the lobby of her building. He thought of all the flowers he'd bought for all the women who'd ever been in his life. Carelessly, impulsively, he'd given roses dozens of times. The single rose he'd bought for Nora was different. Not just a gesture, it meant something to him. He had only to look down at her walking beside him to know that she felt the same.

They reached the elevator, and he asked, "Shall I come up with you?"

She gave the answer he expected. "I don't think so. It's late, I'm exhausted, and I'm sure you're tired of taking care of me."

"No, I'm not. I'll never be tired of that." He leaned forward and kissed her gently, very gently. "You're right, though. It's late, and you'll have a full day tomorrow. I'll be thinking about you, and I'll call."

"Thanks, David, for everything. I can face tomorrow now." Nora kissed him on the cheek before she stepped into the elevator.

He watched as the doors closed and, for a long time afterward, standing there staring into space, his mind was filled with her.

When he walked back to the street, everything seemed to have come alive again. The quiet little world they'd occupied outside her building was suddenly filled with people, laughing and talking as if the two of them hadn't just been there sharing something wonderful. David was almost surprised that the crowds didn't stop to look at him, noticing something different. His feelings must be showing on his face.

But no one stopped except a cabdriver, who pulled up beside him as David stood on the curb, not sure what to do next, which way to go.

"Taxi, buddy?"

"No, thanks," David said as he turned south, finally getting his bearings. "I think I'll walk."

NORA WENT DOWN THE HALL to the kitchen, where she turned on the light and searched through the cabinets until she found just what she wanted, a long-stemmed crystal vase. She trimmed the rose at an angle, pinched off a couple of leaves and put it in the vase, which she filled with tepid water. Then she took it into the office, left it on her desk and turned out the light.

In her bedroom, Nora undressed and turned down the covers but didn't get into bed. She went back into the office and retrieved the rose, then put it on her night table before climbing wearily into bed. Resting her head on the pillow, she could smell its sweet scent.

As she turned off the light, Nora's fingers brushed against the bright red velvety petals. When her rose lost its freshness, she would press it and keep it as a memento of their fledgling relationship. The first memento. A keepsake.

The day that had held so much for Nora included a future that for Phillip was uncertain at best. But she knew that no matter what happened, David would be there. This was just the beginning.

5

NORA AWOKE to the sweet scent of the rose beside her bed and realized she'd been dreaming of David. She stretched, arms high above her head, then relaxed into the pillows, letting his image invade her completely. Just hours before she'd been in his arms, and it had felt so right, so natural to be there.

She knew David wanted her, and there was no denying the feelings he'd aroused in her—that sudden need for him to be even closer. It was exhilarating. It was unexpected and in a way frightening, like being on the edge of a powerful, surging wave. If she let herself go . . .

Yet the time was wrong, she told herself. There was too much else to occupy Nora's life now and for a long time to come, how long she couldn't anticipate. In fact, she couldn't even think past this moment, when she should be preparing the guest room for her father to take over. No time for stretching and lying around in bed, no time, either, for thoughts of David. Her father would be here in an hour, and considering the anticipation with which he'd discussed his plans, Nora fully expected him to be early.

LATE THAT MORNING, Janice arrived in a whirlwind of activity, took her place on the floor and let out an exaggerated moan. "I always beg for outside chores, but today was unreal, although I did find one gift that should be just right."

"Good," Nora said without enthusiasm.

Janice looked up from her purchase. "What's the matter? Oh, I know what's the matter," she answered her own question. "You saw your father last night. Tell. Tell all."

Nora crossed the room to her desk, sat down heavily in the chair and proceeded to inform Janice, as briefly and with as little emotion as possible, of just what had transpired between her father and her.

"I don't believe it," Janice interjected from time to time, at first sadly and then in wonder and finally in amazement. "He's moving in *here*?"

Nora sighed. "That's what I said Janice, but there's actually more. He's already moved in."

"I don't believe it," she repeated.

"Believe it. It's true."

"Nora, I hate to sound callous, particularly considering your father's illness. It's awful, just awful, and I know you're upset. But . . ."

Nora raised her eyebrows and waited.

Janice lowered her voice to a whisper. "You haven't even seen him in fifteen years and suddenly he's moved in. This is a pretty small apartment for the three of us."

Nora couldn't help laughing. "Remember that you don't live here, Janice," she said firmly but lovingly.

"I'm here all day, though. You're here all day. Is he going to be here all day, too?"

"I wish I knew," was all Nora could say. "Whatever happens, he's all settled in, so I'm going to meet David for lunch."

"And leave me here?" Janice looked panic-stricken. "Suppose he comes into the office while you're gone?"

"I'll depend on you to be your usual delightful self."

"Oh, no, Nora, I couldn't—"

"Yes, you could. He's neither a god nor a devil, just a middle-aged man whom you'll probably find quite charming. Don't worry about it, anyway, because Phillip has had a long trip and a couple of hectic days at a hotel. He's resting now, and I'll be back long before he gets up."

DAVID WAS WAITING FOR HER at their usual table at Darcy's. He'd skipped a very important meeting to be here, but amazed as his staff had been when told they'd have to carry on without him, David wasn't fazed by his own decision. He'd make it again if Nora needed him. Even if she didn't need him, he was prepared to cancel any number of meetings just to be with her. Such an attitude about his work had never overcome David before. On the contrary, he'd never considered taking as much as five minutes out of his schedule for any woman. Obviously Nora was special. Last night had told him that much, it had also told him that she shared his feelings, and that made all the difference.

As she walked toward him through the restaurant, weaving gracefully among the close-packed tables,

David could tell from the glow on her face that she still carried with her some of the memory of last night.

Then she saw David and knew there would be something different about their lunch today, something more intimate, more personal. Even though they would talk not of themselves but of Phillip, expressing her anxieties could only bring her closer to David.

It did. There was a shared concern that gave Nora the feeling that she could take care of anything, handle any situation, with his encouragement.

"Phillip seems to be stronger now," she told David. "I still insist that he rest during the day, but he says he gets his energy just from being around me."

"You're probably the best medicine he could have. Has he seen a doctor in New York yet?"

"The clinic in Switzerland recommended a specialist here, but the physician wants to see the medical records from Europe before he sets up an appointment. Meanwhile Phillip says there's nothing that can be done. I suggested he see my doctor, but you know Phillip." She shrugged and managed a little smile. "The top specialist in New York or no one."

Nora looked across the table at David's concerned face. "I can't believe I'm discussing my father's health, when I've hardly thought of him in years. I'd actually gotten used to the fact that I'd never see Phillip again, and now here he is living with me."

"It's going to take some adjustments, Nora. Just having him underfoot will be difficult enough."

Nora smiled almost nervously. "That's what Janice was telling me. If it wasn't so sad, it would be funny, thinking about the three of us falling all over one another. It's a spacious apartment, but not when two of the three are trying to run a business. I don't know whether to laugh or cry, but this sure is going to take some adapting on all our parts."

"I have a feeling your father adapts quite easily," David said, not without a little irritation. "As for Janice, she'll probably fall under his spell, since he's apparently quite a charmer. It's you I'm worried about, Nora. But I'm here. Bring your problems to me," he said, and his look was one of such absolute concern, such caring, that Nora felt the tears begin to well in her eyes.

"I can take care of everything for you," he went on, and she realized David believed what he said. Listening to him, she almost believed, too.

"I can't be calling on you all the time. After all, you're a busy man, an important architect."

"I'll always have time for you," he said, and knew that was true. "I have to fly up to Toronto for a meeting tomorrow, but when I get back, I want to meet him, Nora. I'll understand much more after getting to know your father."

"Maybe, but he's hard to figure out. I don't think anyone has ever really known Phillip."

"Let me give it a try. I may be able to succeed where others have failed," he said confidently. As he reached for her hand, Nora suddenly felt her troubles vanish—at least for the moment.

Fortified by David's encouragement and help, she returned to the apartment ready to face Phillip when he awoke from his nap. She should have known there'd be a surprise in store. From the look of things, he'd been up for some time and had completely taken over the office. A buffet lunch was spread out on the sideboard, and he and Janice were seated cross-legged on the floor, plates heaped high in front of them.

"It's shrimp salad, your favorite," Phillip said as Nora walked into the room. "Please, join us. We decided to eat in here so Janice wouldn't have to leave the phones," he went on to explain, not by way of apology, however. Phillip thought it was perfectly all right, Nora realized, to make himself at home anywhere in the apartment. He'd already taken over physically, and now he was doing so emotionally, by reminding Nora of her childhood. "Remember how I used to make this for you in the summer, and we'd have our lunch on the side porch?"

Suddenly, achingly, Nora remembered. For an instant she was a little girl again, sitting in the middle of the green wooden swing that creaked with age on the screened porch, a plate of shrimp in her lap. Nearby Phillip and Margaret sat in the green porch chairs, talking softly, their voices drifting toward her on the hot midday air, mixing with the lazy buzz of the bees in the roses.

Nora pushed the memories away and tried to replace the closeness that Phillip was seeking with the distance she needed. "I'm sure the salad is as good as ever, but I've already eaten." She sat down at her desk. "I'm glad to see you two are getting to know each other," she felt compelled to add. She *was* glad about that, even though she hadn't doubted the outcome for a moment, Phillip being the charmer he was.

Nora took a quick look at her father, so at home in his unaccustomed position on the floor, laughing and enjoying himself thoroughly. He was wearing light gray trousers and a white shirt open at the neck. A bright blue scarf was knotted at his throat, his signature. Phillip had never liked ties. He always said they were too stiff, too serious for a man of his happy nature. He had amassed a collection of scarves and ascots that filled several drawers.

Despite the ups and downs of his life and the illness that plagued him now, Phillip looked none the worse for wear. Grudgingly, Nora had to admire him. He was a survivor.

"Where did you get the shrimp?" That was about all Nora could find to ask.

"The Fulton Fish Market," Phillip replied.

Nora was amazed. "You've been all the way down there, come back and fixed lunch since I left?"

"Of course," he replied easily. "I couldn't stand the idea of napping in the daytime, and Janice was perfectly willing to forgo her pastrami sandwich for something a little more appetizing."

Janice spoke up between mouthfuls of salad. "It's delicious, Nora. I can imagine why you liked it so much as a child." She must have caught the somewhat scolding look on her boss's face, because she finished the last forkful quickly. "I guess it's time to clean up and get back to work."

"Let me help you," Phillip said, taking both their plates and heading for the kitchen. "I'll come back for the rest."

True to his word, he reappeared to clear off the sideboard, still chatting animatedly. "Janice was telling me all about the Keepsakes office. It's fascinating, especially to an old collector like me."

"He took a call when I was on the other phone and got an order from old Mrs. Bishop," Janice said with excitement. "You know how it usually takes days for her to decide what she wants. Well, your dad gave her a couple of ideas, and she settled on one of them immediately. It was amazing," Janice added with admiration. "Not only that, but it's a simple request, an ivory broach with gold filigree. Maurice has several to choose from."

"They're not very unusual but often very impressive," Phillip added with a little glint in his eye, and Nora realized that something was happening that she hadn't even anticipated, although she certainly should have. It was so like Phillip. Nora was in charge of a profitable business, and her father was inching his way into it.

"Well, I'll just take the rest of these dishes into the kitchen and leave you lovely ladies to your work," he said quickly, aware, Nora expected, that he may have overstepped, moved too fast.

"Your assistant is not only efficient and knowledgeable, she's also very pretty," Phillip said as he exited the room, adding over his shoulder, "you're very lucky, but then so is she."

He disappeared, and Nora sat looking after him silently, avoiding eye contact with Janice, who finally offered meekly, "Did I do something wrong?" When she didn't get a response she added quickly, "I know we shouldn't have had lunch in here, but it seemed so much simpler than using the dining room, and he really wanted to make that salad, Nora." Still no response, so she forged ahead. "Maybe I shouldn't have let him take that call. Mrs. Bishop seemed charmed, though, and I thought—"

"Don't worry about it, Janice. None of this is your fault. It's all to be expected. You'll just have to bear with me for a while. I need some time to get used to becoming an instant daughter."

The phone rang, and Janice reached for it. "Great," she said after a moment. "The boss will be pleased." The look on Janice's face told Nora that she was relieved to find *something* that would please the boss. "Maurice has a tea set that he thinks Mrs. Ashburn will love."

"Thank heavens," Nora said, finally putting her work back in perspective and in place of her father. "Tell him I'll be right over."

"I'll go get it, Nora," Janice offered.

"No, thanks. I want to. Besides," she added right away, trying to keep the desire to get out of the apartment from her voice, "Mrs. Ashburn wasn't very specific in her description, but I know what she has in mind."

"And only you can match her tastes," Janice added.

"I'll admit that's true." Then into the receiver she said, "The boss will be right over."

"THIS JUST WASN'T A DAY for miracles, Maurice," Nora said as she joined him in his office at the back of the shop.

The tea set was on his desk. "It's Limoges just as she wanted, 1800s just as she wanted, pink flowers . . ."

"I know, just as she wanted, but it's not right, Maurice. The colors have to be more pastel, more subdued. I've seen a set exactly like the one Mrs. Ashburn is trying to describe, but if I give her this one, I guarantee she'll be disappointed."

"Well, obviously I don't *want* to lose the sale or commission, but if you know where the one she wants can be found, why in heaven's name don't you buy it?"

"It's not all that easy." Nora relaxed on the comfortable, overstuffed sofa. Maurice sat opposite her, perched on the edge of a Queen Anne chair he used at his desk, why Nora never knew. It was very pretty but certainly not comfortable.

"The set's in Paris?" Maurice guessed.

"No, although I'm sure I could find one like it there, but it would hardly be worth the trip. It's in New Orleans."

"Which would easily be worth the trip. Why don't you fly down and pick it up?"

Nora was thoughtful. "I'm not sure the owner will part with it."

"Oh, my dear, for enough money any owner will part with any keepsake. You know that. And Mrs. Ashburn is filthy rich," he added unnecessarily.

"And Miss Lila is not."

"Miss Lila?" Maurice chuckled. "That's *so* Southern."

"Yes, it is, and she is, but she's never been interested in selling the set. Of course she has her financial ups and downs, so I'm going to try."

"And if the answer is yes, I'd be happy to fly down for you."

"So would Janice," Nora commented, "but this one is mine. I have the feeling it's time for me to get away from New York for a day or two."

NORA STEPPED OFF the streetcar on St. Charles Avenue and headed down Laudelet toward the river. Lila Rhodes, an old friend of Nora's since her childhood days in New Orleans, had agreed to sell the French tea set. Nora had leaped at the opportunity to leave New York, especially since business was slow at Keepsakes and David was in Canada. Neither of those was the real reason she was walking down this New Orleans street, though, and Nora knew it.

She'd come here to try to get away from Phillip. Not that he'd been any real trouble. After the first day he hadn't insinuated himself into the business of running the office again, keeping himself at arm's length and being overly polite. Jet lag and fatigue had finally caught up with him, he'd spent much of his time resting in his room. But he'd be back. He'd come to life again. Of that Nora was certain, and she needed this trip to afford her the space, the time to assess their situation.

What better place to do that than in New Orleans, the city where she was born, where she grew up as Phillip Chase's daughter, where they'd last been together. It was a beautiful city full of scents that belonged to New Orleans alone, the river, the late-blooming flowers, the hint of rain that seemed always in the clouds even on a sunny day, the heavy, fragrant air. She took a deep breath. No place in the world smelled quite like it, and as far as Nora was concerned, the taste of New Orleans was unmatched. She'd stepped off the plane with a yearning for Cajun food, and she planned to satisfy that yearning later in the evening. But the afternoon belonged to Miss Lila.

The house was well set back from the street, a large frame home dating from the turn of the century. The wraparound front porch was decorated with familiar curlicues of that era, and if the railings were showing some wear, that was to be expected. A few of them tilted to one side, one or two were missing, and they all needed painting badly, but the shopworn look only added to the house's charm. The yard made up for the other signs of neglect. It burst forth on the senses in a riot of color, the impatiens and begonias not yet faded by autumn.

Nora climbed the steps and rang the bell. Almost at once the door was flung open, and she was enveloped in a hug.

"My dear child, how wonderful to see you."

Nora hugged back, inhaling another achingly memorable scent, that of lavender and silk, of old ladies in cool parlors, tea and sherry and memories, a flood of memories that brought tears to her eyes.

Lila Rhodes was still as tall and erect as ever, almost regal in her carriage. The wrinkles on her pale face had proliferated, but the bright blue eyes shone with the fervor Nora remembered as Lila stood back and admired her young friend.

"I'm so glad to see you in New Orleans again at last. All this communication by mail and telephone is just not satisfying." She held Nora away from her. "You're lovelier than ever."

"And so are you," Nora said, admiring the gray, beautifully coiffed hair and black lacy dress that was perfect on Miss Lila's slim frame. It was from an era Nora remembered, long past, but the dress was still stylish when worn with such flair. "You look wonderful."

Lila's reaction to the compliment was a burst of laughter. "I'm just an old woman," she said as she took Nora's arm and led her into the parlor, but her step was sprightly, and she seemed much younger than her years, which Nora calculated must be well over seventy.

"You know the three ages of women, don't you?" When Nora shook her head Lila informed her, "Youth, middle age and 'you look wonderful'!" She chuckled delightedly.

"In your case it's not a joke," Nora insisted as she sat down in the big old parlor that was also just as she'd recalled, if not a little more crammed with antiques and objets d'art. The chair that Nora had chosen was one she remembered well, the upholstery a little more worn, the tiny flowers somewhat faded. As a child her feet hadn't touched the floor when she'd sat there in her party dress, eating biscuits hot from the oven.

"That was your favorite chair," Lila observed. "It could use a face-lift. Like everything and everyone in this house," she joked again.

"I like it just as it is," Nora said, letting herself relax into the room that was a hodgepodge of Victoriana mixed with scattered French pieces, all the inheritance from relatives whom Lila Rhodes had outlived.

Belongings rather than money had been passed along through this New Orleans family, and what little income Lila had was eaten up by the old house that was a mausoleum to heat in the winter or to cool in the summer. When the roof sprang a leak or a pipe burst, that's when Miss Lila would call on Nora and sell an heirloom. It had turned into a profitable and satisfying arrangement for both of them.

"I thought we'd let the tea set pass from hand to hand in a little ceremony," Lila said, rolling out a tea cart. On it were crustless round sandwiches covered with a linen cloth, tiny iced cakes and a variety of cookies.

The tea set was as beautiful as Nora had remembered. She picked up one of the delicate, hand-painted cups. The china was paper thin, with a gold leaf handle and pale pink and green flowers. "This is exactly what my client wants," Nora said, relieved that she'd been able to rely on her memory, since her client could not. "Mrs. Ashburn had trouble explaining exactly what the tea set looked like."

"Then how do you know this is the one?" Lila asked.

"I just know," Nora answered confidently. "But even if I'm wrong, she'll like this so much that she'll think it's the one." Nora laughed. "You have to know her to understand."

"Thank heavens I can leave that to you. I'm afraid I just couldn't cope with the whims of buyers." Lila poured the tea and handed a cup to Nora. "Jasmine, your favorite."

"You remembered."

"Well, of course I remembered. You grew up a block away, after all, Nora. I remember many things about you. Sugar?"

"Please."

"I remember that, too. You always took a heaping spoonful."

"Still do." Nora lifted the top of the sugar bowl and then paused, admiring again the exquisite shape and design of the china.

"I wouldn't sell this set if I were you. It's incredibly lovely, Miss Lila."

"Oh, I know," Miss Lila said. "It's been in the family for generations. My great-grandmother LaFont brought it over from France as part of her dowry in the fifties. The 1850s, that is," she added with a laugh.

"I don't feel right about buying it," Nora said hesitantly. "So many family memories."

"It's only a tea set, Nora," Lila reprimanded her. "I can part with it and still keep my memories." She took a sip of tea and looked critically at the cup. "Frankly, dear, I don't think it's all that grand. If someone else can get pleasure from it, so be it." She put down her cup and leaned close to Nora. "So name your price. What's the bottom line?"

It was Nora's turn to laugh.

"I have to admit that I've gone a little into the red again," Miss Lila confessed.

"Not more problems with the house?" Nora asked with concern.

"Not this time, though I'd better knock on wood. But I did run up a little bill at Galatoire's last month that I need to take care of."

"Bridge club?" Nora asked, familiar with Lila's lifestyle.

"It was my turn as hostess, and I could have had the cook come in and prepare a nice luncheon, but we were celebrating a very important birthday, the eightieth," she added in a whisper, "of one of our founding members, so I decided on Galatoire's. I had no idea the girls would order so many courses or drink so much of the best wine. Yes," she added thoughtfully, "I definitely need to replenish my coffers."

Nora mentioned a price that made Lila's eyes sparkle.

"Hmm, I just might sell everything in the house if you're offering that kind of money."

"No," Nora said, "I won't let you. These are your treasures, a part of your heritage. I'd give anything to have some keepsakes from my past."

Lila's eyes softened. "You do, my dear," she said caringly. "Yours may not be tangible, but you have memories of your childhood, and most of them are happy."

"Until I was sixteen," Nora reminded her older friend.

"Yes, until then, but everyone must grow up eventually. You just had to do so a little early, that's all. But think of the years before that, the three of you in that beautiful old home. And the parties. I'll never forget them, some of New Orleans's finest. Invitations were sought after. Phillip loved a good party. He also loved his family, both Margaret and you. That's true, Nora," she chided gently.

"I know," Nora admitted. "I've been thinking about that a great deal recently." She took a deep breath and then let the news escape. "He's back, Miss Lila. Phillip is in New York."

"Great balls of fire!" Lila exclaimed. "After all this time. Well, how is the rapscallion?"

Some sixth sense told Nora not to blurt out the news of her father's illness. "He looks well," she said, which was certainly true. "He seems determined to catch up on the lost years."

"And you?"

"I'm going to try, but it's very difficult for me. So much time has passed."

"Indeed, it has."

"He's living with me, at least for now." Even as she spoke, Nora had to struggle with the reality of it.

"Well, I'm not sure how I feel about that," Lila said as she poured herself another cup of the strong tea.

Nora had to laugh. "I'm not sure myself."

"He's a very complicated man and difficult to live with, I think." She smiled a little sadly. "I don't just think—I know. Your mother had a hard time of it." Lila was silent for a moment and then began to reminisce.

"He was much younger than I, but I remember Phillip quite well, even as a child. A handsome boy, but something of a hellion. When he grew up, he channeled some of that spirit into a winning personality."

Nora listened quietly, knowing this was one of the reasons she'd come back, to hear about her father from one who knew him well.

"Just like most women—and most men, for that matter—I enjoyed being around your father. He could always make me laugh. As for the girls his age, well, he turned quite a few heads, your mother's among them. She was determined to marry him. Margaret set her cap for that boy, and even though they were obviously ill suited, she persisted."

"You never told me that."

"You never asked, my dear. In fact, you never wanted to talk about Phillip at all, and I can't blame you because of the hurt you carried. But you're older now and wiser, I'm sure, wise enough to understand that Margaret and Phillip were a very unusual couple and theirs a very unusual marriage."

"That's certainly true," Nora said wryly.

"Your father was an adventurer, which both fascinated and frightened Margaret, but it didn't stop her. I might add that she knew exactly what she was getting into. The future was predictable, and it didn't look good."

"But she married him, anyway," Nora mused.

"She loved him. Now, in those days, in this part of the world, when you got married you stayed married. Except I think Margaret was different. If Phillip hadn't left, she would have kicked him out eventually. She was as strong willed as he."

"I always wished they had stayed together."

"Good Lord, child, that would have been disaster. As it happened, everything turned out for the best."

At Nora's puzzled look, she went on, "You were forced to get out on your own and make something of yourself. And look at the result, a beautiful, successful woman with a wonderful life and career."

"Oh, Miss Lila, you really know how to make me feel good."

"'Course I do, by telling the truth." Lila passed a plate of sandwiches and smiled lovingly. "This is like old times, isn't it. You come over in the afternoon for a tea party..."

"And you tell me all the gossip. Who's engaged, who's in love, which girl got called out by which boy at the carnival balls. I miss hearing the gossip."

"Well, there's no reason why we can't catch up."

For the next hour Lila regaled her guest with tales of New Orleans society, some of which Nora was sure were invented on the spot, but all of which were fascinating. It was almost five o'clock when Nora helped clear the table and offered to do the dishes.

"No such thing. I'll wash the tea set carefully and pack it in a nice box with lots of tissue paper."

"I'll come by in the morning," Nora said, aware that both she and Lila wanted as much time together as possible.

"There's really no reason why you can't stay here with me," Lila said as they walked to the door. "I'm dining with friends, but I can easily call and ask them to set another place."

"No," Nora said. "I enjoy staying in the French Quarter, and I wouldn't want to intrude on your plans. Besides," she added truthfully, "I'm looking forward to a real Cajun meal."

"That's right," Lila said, "you always liked jambalaya and fried fish."

"And I haven't had a meal like that in years."

"All right, I'll let you indulge yourself, but when you come back, luncheon will be very, very French. Don't forget the other New Orleans tradition."

"Never." Nora laughed. She gave a final goodbye wave to Lila and went down the steps to the flower-infested walk. The sky was darkening, and the breeze had freshened everything. But the clouds hung very low in the sky, filled with the threat of rain.

Nora reached the corner and stopped. With just a short detour, she could walk by the old Chase house on St. John Street. It wasn't far at all, less than five minutes. She hesitated for a long time before stepping off the curb and heading for the streetcar.

She'd had enough of the past today; it was time to face the future, and the future was in New York. The future was Phillip. She'd run away from him by coming to New Orleans, but she couldn't run anymore. She had to start making plans for what remained of his future. Somehow they were going to have to work out a relationship. Nora was willing, she told herself, but she needed time. It wasn't her nature to rush into anything.

The rain started before Nora got back to her hotel in the French Quarter. Soaking wet, she crossed the lobby of the Petite Auberge and, leaving watery footprints, made her way down the hall to her room. Once inside, she stripped off her clothes and took a long shower. With the rain and darkness there was a sudden taste of fall in the air, and Nora was glad she'd brought her heavy terry-cloth robe. She slipped into it and began to dry her hair.

Even though she should have been concentrating on the future, Nora kept thinking of the past, of Lila's comments about Phillip and Margaret. They had loved each other once, of that she was sure. Even though she'd always blamed him for leaving, she knew the blame wasn't his alone. Margaret had been demanding and childlike in many ways. For that matter, so had Phillip. What a mismatch, Nora thought. What strange things love does and what odd couples it makes.

She tossed the towel into the bathroom and ran her fingers through her dark brown hair. It still wasn't dry, and Nora was in a hurry. The rain had stopped as suddenly as it had begun, and through her window she could see the lights of the French Quarter beckoning to her. She plugged in her hair dryer; in less than ten minutes she'd styled her hair and put on her makeup. She wanted to do a great deal of exploring in the Quarter before dinner and maybe again afterward. It had been a long, long time.

She was just reaching for her clothes, when someone knocked on the door. She opened it a crack, leaving the chain on. "Yes—" she began.

"It's David. I've come to take you to dinner."

6

DAVID HELD UP HIS HAND in a gesture of supplication. "Before you say a word, let me explain."

Nora withheld a smile, but with difficulty. She was anxious to hear what kind of explanation he came up with.

"When I returned from Canada, Janice told me you were on a business trip."

"Hmm."

David persisted. "I'm sure she couldn't have imagined at first that I was planning to follow, so she gladly told me that you were in New Orleans." He paused, but Nora was silent. "When I asked the hotel's name, she became a little suspicious."

"I imagine she did." Nora also imagined that Janice was as much excited as suspicious. She adored the thought of romance blossoming between her boss and the architect.

"I had to bribe her to get all the information," David insisted. "She didn't want to give it out."

Nora couldn't suppress a smile at that, but she held back a doubtful comment.

"So don't be angry with her."

"I'm not angry with either of you, David. I'm just surprised. What in the world are you doing here?"

"I told you. I've come to take you to dinner. In the meantime, I wonder if you'd mind letting me in?" he asked in a boyishly pleading tone. The whole conversation had taken place through the half-opened door, and David had begun to attract the attention of other guests passing in the hall.

"Of course. I don't know what I was thinking." Nora opened the door wide, but when David stepped into her room, she reached instinctively for the neck of her robe, drawing it closer. "I've just had a shower," she explained, obviously a little flustered.

"That's apparent," David said. He couldn't help staring, even though he saw that Nora was uneasy. There was simply no way to keep his eyes off her. He moved a step back so that she would relax. He'd never seen Nora with her hair down, its dark glossy brown waves hanging to her shoulders. The fading light that filtered through the window seemed to caress her hair, but when she moved out of the light, the sheen remained. Flattering light wasn't necessary to illuminate Nora.

"I like your hair down," he said, and as he spoke he couldn't help reaching out and touching the dark waves. After that it was easy to let his hand drift to her cheek and stay there. He wanted to lean forward, close the space between them and kiss her. Though he wanted that very much, he stopped himself. She was obviously uneasy, not just because he'd turned up on her doorstep when she'd least expected, but because of the intimacy of the hotel bedroom, and because she was dressed in her robe with nothing beneath it but bare skin.

"I hope you haven't had dinner," he said. He'd dropped his hand from her cheek, but neither of them had moved.

"No, I haven't."

"Good. I'm starved. I skipped dinner on the plane so I could have a good New Orleans meal."

"Where would you like to go?" she asked.

"This is your town. You be my guide to good dining."

"How about a muffeleta?"

"What in the world is that?" he asked.

"A New Orleans-style sandwich—like a hoagie or a submarine."

David was already shaking his head. "I'm hungry, Nora, and a sandwich won't do."

"French food?"

"What about something more basic?"

Nora nodded. She'd given him other choices, and now she was ready to offer the kind of meal she'd been looking forward to all day. "Cajun?"

"That's it," David said. "Authentic Cajun food sounds like just the thing. But only if you agree."

"I can be persuaded," she said with a knowing smile. "I'll need a few minutes to get dressed."

David sat down in a chair by the window, crossing his arms. "Mind if I wait?"

Nora raised her eyebrows and gave a little shake of her head, letting David know that her uneasiness had fled. Then she picked up her dress and stepped into the bathroom.

Leaning back in his chair, David pulled the draperies open wide and looked out onto the patio. Raindrops glistened on the fountain and the surrounding plants. It was very different here from New York, with a sort of wildness and abandon in the lush foliage and also in the spirit of the people. He'd noticed the difference on the way to the hotel, and now he noticed it again. It was very pleasing to him somehow.

David thought about his return from Canada to New York, the drive into Manhattan, the phone call to Janice and the almost immediate return to the airport. When he thought about it, he realized he was as surprised as Nora that he'd turned up in New Orleans. It certainly hadn't been planned, but when he'd talked to Janice and wheedled Nora's whereabouts out of her, he'd gotten additional information that concerned him. Janice had let it slip that Nora was so uneasy with Phillip that she'd actually fled to New Orleans.

He'd considered that for only a few moments before realizing that Nora was troubled and needed company. More important, David believed that she needed *him*.

She didn't look as if she needed him when she opened the door and stepped into the room. She was wearing a gray turtleneck sweater-dress with ribbing from about the middle of her thigh to the hemline and a big pocket just above the hip. It was made of a lightweight material that was very tempting. Once more he wanted to reach out and touch her. Best of all, she was still wearing her hair down, but just as he started to comment on that, she turned to the mirror, brushing it back from her face.

While David watched, she twisted the thick strands into a bun, which she pinned at her nape. He felt little twinges of pain with each hairpin that anchored the bun, and he longed to stop her, take out the pins and let her hair fall back down again into his waiting hands. It took all his willpower to remain seated and comment in a tone that he tried to keep casual, "You look lovely."

Nora turned then, and his heart skipped a beat at her smile. "Thank you," she said softly.

"Where are we going?" he asked, still not taking his eyes off her.

"I thought it would be fun to take you to a restaurant called Nettie and André's, and don't ask me how two people with such different names got together. He's pure Cajun."

"And what about Nettie?"

"She came to the Bayou Country from somewhere in the Midwest, I think, but she does wonders with Cajun herbs and spices. Anyway, the two of them are a New Orleans institution. I've looked forward to this visit ever since I got to New Orleans."

"Aha. So this is a setup? You led me into asking for Cajun food."

Nora laughed. "Exactly. Thanks for having such wonderful taste." She stood on tiptoe and kissed his cheek. "And thanks for being here tonight. I didn't know it, but I needed someone to talk to."

David's arms went around her for a moment and held her close. He could feel her warm skin through the light fabric of her dress, just as he'd imagined but even more exciting. Briefly he considered what she'd say if he suggested forgetting dinner, the Cajun food, Nettie and André, all of New Orleans, and staying in her room. That's what he really wanted, to spend the whole evening with her, just the two of them.

"I thought you were starving," she reminded David when he showed no inclination to move.

He tightened his arms around her waist. "I've almost forgotten that particular appetite."

"Jambalaya?" Getting no reaction, she continued, "Okra gumbo, crayfish hush puppies . . ."

"All right," he said, releasing her reluctantly. "You've sold me."

"We'll find a cozy corner and have lots of time to talk."

"Lead on," he said. "I'm right behind you."

NETTIE AND ANDRÉ'S was everything Nora had promised. Tucked away on a quiet street in the French Quarter, the restaurant had interior walls of old brick with exposed beams. The tabletops were wooden and scarred from use. As hoped, they found a quiet corner, but it wasn't quiet for long.

André appeared from behind the counter, his big belly preceding him, his many chins trembling with excitement. "I recognized you the minute you walked in, little Nora. How many years has it been?"

"Many years, André, but you haven't changed a bit."

"A little fatter maybe, but you are the same . . . only more beautiful."

While David watched and listened, the two reminisced about the old days and Phillip Chase, with André citing Phillip's good taste in food as well as everything else.

When the chef left, David commented, "The ubiquitous Phillip."

Nora agreed. "I can't seem to avoid him by leaving my apartment. Of course, most of the memories are here in New Orleans. Miss Lila and I spent a long time talking about him this afternoon." Nora was momentarily pensive. "I learned some things I hadn't known before."

"Maybe you asked some questions you hadn't asked before," David suggested.

"Yes, I did, and Miss Lila was more than willing to answer them."

"I assume this Miss Lila also has something to do with the business part of your reason for coming to New Orleans."

"Yes. She's an old family friend and has agreed to sell a very rare tea set I've been trying to find for one of my clients."

Their first course of seafood gumbo was finished in record time, and Nettie arrived with their second course, stuffed catfish for David and soft-shell crabs for Nora. Conversation about Keepsakes, even thoughts of it, were put aside.

They were silent for a long time, enjoying their meal, sharing bites with each other and then agreeing on an extra order of fried oysters.

"I'm glad your appetite is as big as mine," David said.

"It's unending," Nora managed between bites.

When they finally finished the meal and Nettie brought their coffee, David commented again on Nora's trip. "I can't imagine you'll make enough money on the sale of the tea set to justify flying down here."

"Actually, I'll come out ahead, but the real profit comes later."

David quirked an eyebrow.

"It all has to do with public relations. If I fail to locate what Mrs. Ashburn wants, then I start losing credibility." Nora took a sip of the strong coffee. "When I lose credibility, Keepsakes loses customers. As it is, my client will be so thrilled with this set—and with its past—that she'll continue her requests and recommend me to all her friends."

"You *are* a good businesswoman," he said admiringly.

"I try, but it's not always easy."

"I can imagine, and it's probably less so these days, with your father around." David had managed to slide naturally into talking about Phillip.

Nora sighed. "I'm still not sure I did the right thing by inviting him to live with me."

"I don't think you had any alternative, Nora. You couldn't turn your back on him."

"I'm just not ready to share so much of my life. You know that's difficult for me, being close." Her eyes slid away from his.

David smiled and reached for her hand. "*We're* making progress, aren't we?"

She still didn't meet his eyes.

"Aren't we, Nora?"

Finally she looked up at him. "Yes," she admitted.

"Not as much as I'd like—" he left the thought dangling "—but progress, just the same."

She was still looking directly at him. That last observation hadn't made her flinch.

"You know how much I care about you," David said, taking advantage of the moment. "How much I want you."

Nora felt her heart accelerate. David had always been devastatingly direct. It was exciting and flattering. It was also a little frightening. She'd gotten over her momentary embarrassment and was more at ease than she'd been when the conversation had begun, but her relaxed state was nothing compared to his.

David was leaning toward her, his chin cupped in his palm, watching her with easy, admiring eyes, a half smile on his face. The candlelight played along the clean lines of his jaw, and Nora was suddenly aware of his strong good looks. She let herself get lost in his unbelievable blue eyes and didn't allow thoughts to go beyond tonight, being there with him.

"I see you're not going to answer me," he observed.

"I've forgotten the question," Nora admitted, and they both laughed.

"It wasn't really a question," David said. "More of an observation."

"Oh, yes, about us," Nora said, remembering. "I don't really know how to respond, David. I only know that I can't be pushed."

"You don't have to worry about that," he promised. "Now—" leaning back in his chair, he glanced at the menu "—what are the choices for dessert?"

Nora was about to object, when he named something she couldn't resist. "Here's the very thing. Ambrosia and pralines."

"Do we dare?" Nora asked, sure his answer would suit her.

"Of course. And afterward, let's take in the night-life. I've traveled all over the world, but this is my first time in New Orleans, so I don't plan to miss a thing."

Nora was suddenly very tired, but she didn't want to disappoint David, who was apparently good for the night. "We could explore the Quarter."

David heard something in her voice that made him ask, "Are you not feeling up to it?"

"Well, I am a little tired, but since this will be our only night together..."

"Oh, no," he argued. "I plan to stay over another day—and night." There was a twinkle in his eyes. "That is, if you can put up with me. Or maybe you'll be busy with clients and dealers. I didn't even think about that."

"Nothing that can't be put off until the following day." Nora knew it would be easy to rearrange appointments; she also knew it might not be so easy for

David. "But what about you? Can you really afford a nonworkday in the middle of the week?"

"Actually," he admitted, "I thought I'd take a couple of hours to look over the renovation down on the Mississippi riverfront. The architectural firm that designed it studied my East Side project. I'd like to see the results."

Their dessert had arrived, and David was well into the ambrosia. "Delicious," he commented. "But about tomorrow, I wish you'd go with me. I don't think it'll be too boring."

"I'm sure it won't," Nora said, and realized with those words that she'd committed herself.

DAVID TOOK HER HAND, and they walked slowly through the Quarter toward her hotel. The streets were washed fresh and clean from the rain that glistened in the lamplight, giving everything an otherworldly look. Except that it wasn't otherworldly at all, because everywhere they saw throngs of people, tourists pouring out of restaurants and bars, filling the shops that remained open until midnight, creating a kind of carnival atmosphere.

David didn't seem to notice. He had eyes only for her, but Nora wished that somehow the crowds would magically disappear, leaving them alone on the rain-washed streets, alone with the music that filtered from the jazz clubs into the night air.

They turned into a narrow alley that threaded its way behind the Petite Auberge, and suddenly all was quiet. The night *was* theirs alone. Their footsteps echoed along the pavement, and overhead the palmetto fronds rustled in the night breeze. There were no other sounds, and because of the confines of the alley, no other sights except the brick buildings stacked together on either side of them with Old World charm.

The hotel patio was deserted, lit only by a faint stream of light from the office window. Their shadows danced against the rain-splattered bricks and then were still.

David reached out and touched her face, and in the palm of his hand there lingered the fragrant dewiness of night air. She didn't resist the touch. All her senses seemed attuned to the spot on her face where his hand rested. Then he moved his fingers slowly, caressing the jawline, down and around to the back of her neck. Every inch of her skin tingled beneath the slow progression of his hand.

Exerting just the slightest pressure, David drew her closer and closer until their faces were almost touching. She moistened her lips with the tip of her tongue. It was instinctive; she probably hadn't realized she'd done it, but the result sent electric shocks through David's whole body, for their mouths were just close enough that her tongue touched his lips.

Hungrily his mouth pressed against hers, and lips and tongues met in a kiss that was the culmination of their whole evening together, from the moment he'd seen her in the hotel with her hair falling around her face and all the moments afterward. Now he was holding her, holding her....

Her mouth was soft and sweet beneath his, and his tongue sought that sweetness again and again. His arms enclosed Nora and felt her fragility. His hands moved over her and felt her warmth. He imagined what it would be like to touch her skin. He *knew* what it would be like, for beneath her dress she seemed to be on fire. Like hot silk, that's how her skin would feel. He longed for her nakedness beneath him, her slim and yet utterly soft body, free of her clothes, clinging to him.

David's lips left her mouth and traced a damp path down her neck. He felt her shiver; he heard a soft little sound escape her lips. He moved his hand from her back to her shoulder, feeling the suppleness beneath his fingers as they traced the line of her collarbone and slipped lower to cup her breast. He rubbed the palm of his hand lightly over her nipple. She leaned against him, increasing the pressure of his touch, and he knew she felt a passion akin to his own.

It grew and grew within Nora as she clung to him, giving herself to the touch of his hand on her breast and his lips moving over her face as his other hand held her close.

"Nora!" His voice was a whisper on the breeze, and it asked a question, extended a provocative invitation.

She couldn't respond, for she wasn't sure of the answer. Instead she raised her face for his kiss. She wanted him, wanted to be with him, and not just here in the dewy night. Along the length of her body she could feel him, hard, yearning, demanding. It would be so easy to take his hand and cross the space to her room. The wrought-iron gate seemed to beckon to them. Yet she couldn't respond, and she didn't even know why.

Perhaps she couldn't trust herself, or perhaps she couldn't trust David. She wasn't sure of the emotions that were playing within each of them. She was beginning to know how difficult it was for her, at least, to understand those emotions when they concerned David. Everything was so mixed-up, so confused. And especially with David, it was important that each moment between them be right.

She rested her forehead against his shoulder. "Oh, David," she said softly, "I care for you so much."

"I know." He held her tightly. He did know, and the knowledge comforted him even while it excited him. He held her closer.

"I need time," she said. "I need to think."

He'd been afraid that was coming, and in spite of himself, his body tensed against her. "I'm trying to understand, Nora, but I'm not a very patient man. I can't turn off my feelings for you."

"I know that."

She didn't have to move away. David moved first, forcing himself to step back and check his feelings, hold them in abeyance. It wouldn't be easy, but he would do it for her. He took her hand and walked her through the gate that seemed to have beckoned to them before, like the entrance to a romantic dream they could share. But now it was only another gate. He lifted the latch and pushed it open.

"I know you're confused, Nora, not just about me but about your father, about everything that's going on in your life. But I won't let all the other concerns keep us apart. What's happening now is between you and me, Nora. It has nothing to do with Phillip and your running from him."

"I know that."

"He mustn't come between us." There was insistence in David's voice.

"No," she agreed.

"I can't wait much longer."

"I won't ask you to," she promised.

THEIR VISIT WITH LILA was all that Nora could have wished for. A born flirt, Lila found her match in David, and their innuendos kept Nora laughing throughout the meal, which was, as Lila had promised, French from entrée to dessert.

Nora had warned David that her elderly friend never considered taking no for an answer, whatever the question. He found out how true that was.

"I wouldn't have eaten quite so much," David said as they drove away from the house, "except that she kept insisting and I didn't dare decline."

Nora laughed. "I told you she was stubborn."

"Like someone else I know." There was a twinkle in his eye as David looked away from the street long enough to glance over at Nora.

"Maybe there's something in the Garden District water," Nora teased back. She relaxed against the car seat and thought about David and Lila. They had developed a deeper sense of camaraderie than she could have hoped for. Seeing them together had pleased her immensely, but, then, everything about her time in New Orleans with David had been pleasing. Being alone with him outside of New York, seeing him in new situations, just proved how well he fitted in. In many ways she was as comfortable with him here, and in all ways she was more comfortable with him than she'd been with anyone in her life. Just as in New York, David took charge. That wouldn't change from setting to setting.

Suddenly he stopped the car and displayed that side of his nature once more. "Wait a minute," he said. "Weren't you and Lila neighbors when you were growing up?"

"Yes," she answered. "My family lived just around the block from Miss Lila."

"I want to see your house."

"David, I don't think—" Nora had gone through all that the day before and decided against it.

"Yes," he said. "I think it's important for me to see where you spent your childhood. I want to know all about you, Nora, and that was a big part of your life."

She tried again. "I don't think . . ." Not really having an excuse, she manufactured one. "We're already near the hotel. You don't want to drive all that way back."

"Yes, I do," he contradicted. "Even if you've seen the house again, I haven't."

"Neither have I."

David looked at her quizzically. He'd already made a U-turn, but once more he pulled over. "What is it, Nora? Why don't you want to go back?"

Because she didn't know the answer, if there was one, she denied her negativism. "No reason. Let's have a look at the old home place," she said cheerfully.

On the drive back to the Garden District, David talked about Lila again, going over one by one the antiques and artifacts in her house.

"You certainly were observant," Nora told him.

"I was thinking of you."

"I remind you of a Sevres bowl?" she asked him with a grin, "or a Dresden dish?"

"More like a curvaceous Steuben vase. No, what I meant was that she has enough treasures in her house to keep your business going for years."

Nora's answer was so fiercely defensive that it surprised even her. "She's growing old, David, and those treasures, as you call them, are all she has left of the past. She only parts with them when necessity demands it. I'd never take her keepsakes from her. Never."

"I wouldn't want you to," David said, just as determinedly. "I only meant that she might like to share more in your transactions and gain some monetary reward at the same time. She parted with this quite happily." He indicated the box on the seat beside Nora, which held the precious tea set.

"Yes, she seemed to, but I still believe she was more stricken than she let on. It's difficult to lose a keepsake. I know. I lost all of mine."

"They're only things, Nora," he reminded her. "You can hold them in your hand but not in your heart."

"I know," she agreed, and he wondered whether she believed her words or only spoke them to prevent an argument. "Besides, I have my memories—good and bad."

Following her instructions, David turned off St. Charles Avenue and pulled up in front of a large frame house. "What kind of memories do you have now, good or bad?"

Nora looked out the window at the house of her childhood, set back from the street and surrounded by the same trees she remembered. There was a swing hanging from one of the low branches of a live oak. On that same tree, on that same branch, her swing had once dangled. "My memories are good ones," she answered.

There had been some changes. The house was painted light gray with dark blue shutters and awnings. When she was little it had been white and, by the time they'd left, badly in need of a painting. Wicker furniture had replaced the heavy wooden slatted chairs, with their wide armrests, that she'd felt so tiny in as a little girl. The chairs had been painted green, like the shutters on her childhood home.

"Do you want to go in?" David asked. "We could explain who you are, and I'm sure the owners wouldn't mind."

Nora shook her head. "No, I just want to look at it."

A young couple came out of the house, pushing open the screen door, preceded by two children. The little girl ran across the yard. Her father followed, lifted her into the swing and gave it a push to get her started.

Nora smiled to herself. The memories *were* good. "It's still a happy house," she said. "I guess it always was, but I tend to forget that sometimes."

"That's a problem all of us deal with, remembering the bad times instead of the good."

"Well, I'm going to stop dwelling on the past and think only of the present."

"And the future," he suggested as he started the car and drove back down the tree-lined street.

"Yes," she echoed, "the future. Starting right now. No more talk about Phillip or about my memories, or even keepsakes." She looked over at David. He was wearing a polo shirt and a Vee-necked sweater, blue just like his eyes, which were hidden behind sunglasses now, but the color of which she recalled exactly. "I'm sorry about the outburst," she added, "over Miss Lila's keepsakes."

"I don't think she puts the same importance on them that you do," he said gently.

Nora nodded. "I'll try to relegate them to the past, too."

He reached over and touched her hand. "Sounds good to me. Now what's on the agenda for the present?"

"Let's explore the riverfront renewal."

"Fine," he said, "and although I can't think about eating again right now, later on we can have dinner at one of New Orleans's famous restaurants like . . ."

"Arnaud's or the Commander's Palace," she filled in for him.

"Followed by dancing at a romantic spot, which we'll discover along the way."

"A perfect ending to a day I won't forget."

7

"YOU WERE RIGHT," David said huskily. "This is a never-to-be-forgotten day."

Nora nestled her head against his shoulder as they swayed to the music. The little club was deserted except for Nora and David, the three-piece band and a tired bartender, who leaned sleepily against the counter.

David and Nora had arrived more than an hour earlier, when the club was still filled with patrons gathered at tables and on the dance floor. The mood had been upbeat as the trio jammed through request after request. The club was a popular spot, but now the night was winding down into morning. The muted trombone played the melody, the sax a mellow lead and the piano soft background chords while Nora and David, wrapped in each other's arms, were oblivious to everything except the haunting rhythm and the closeness of their bodies.

Their silence was broken now and then by disjointed comments about the day's events, half spoken, sometimes answered and sometimes not. It didn't seem to matter.

"I'm glad you had a chance to look over the river project today," she said at one point.

The remark elicited only a lazy "Hmm."

A few minutes later he answered more completely, "I think the architects did a good job." When she agreed with a nod, he added, "I only apologize for staying so long."

"I enjoyed myself," she murmured against his chest.

"Even though I kept you there all afternoon?" He wrapped his fingers around the back of her neck and touched the fresh flower she'd woven into the twist of her hair.

Nora lifted her head just enough to look at him. "I loved being there with you, sharing the time, hearing your ideas."

"I had quite a few of them, as usual," he admitted. "That's what happens when you let me get on the subject of buildings, old, new—"

"Renovated," she put in.

"Even razed," he said with a laugh. "Just so another one can go up in the same space. I guess I'm a blueprint fanatic."

"The best one around," she told him.

David looked down at her and smiled. His fingers were still caressing the back of her neck. "You're very good for my ego."

There was a pause in the music. The three men on the bandstand looked at one another and shrugged as the pianist struck a chord and another set began, softly.

"You're good for me, too—in so many ways," Nora said. She snuggled her head back into his shoulder.

"I'm glad," he whispered as he dropped a kiss on top of her hair and held her more comfortably, both of them still swaying to the music. His hands moved over the black, silky material of the dress that clung to her so beautifully. For a long time they didn't say anything more, both lost in thought. David was thinking she was the most beautiful woman he'd ever known, thinking how good he'd felt when they'd swept into Arnaud's earlier for dinner. All eyes had been on her. He had felt proud of that. He'd also felt protective, holding on to her arm firmly, possessively. To that feeling of pride, there had been added desire. David had wanted her then, and he wanted her now.

The special world they'd created for themselves hadn't included so much as a mention of Phillip. They'd talked only of each other, spoken only to each other. That had lasted through the night until now when they were truly alone. It was as if the whole world had finally walked away and let them be. Even the musicians were a part of another time, another space, merely background for them. As for the bartender, he was asleep, his head resting comfortably on his folded arms.

They'd almost achieved this magical interlude the night before, but tonight was different. The time was right for them. When David spoke again, it was without hesitation, without foreboding.

"Some good has come out of the turmoil of the past week."

"Hmm," Nora said, not really following his thinking.

"It led to yesterday and today."

"Yes." She understood.

The trombone picked up the melody from the sax and changed the tempo completely, from torrid blues to lilting romance, and with that swing in mood, David added, "I know now how much I need to be with you." In fact, he'd known that almost from the beginning, but he hadn't admitted it to her. "I'm a man who's always been in control, Nora. I make things happen. Now for the first time, I'm involved in something that's out of my hands. What comes next is up to you."

There was still movement in their bodies, but it was motion almost as imperceptible, as slow and romantic as the music itself. "It's more than need, though, Nora," David said, touching her chin with his fingertips so that she was looking at him, seeing deeply into his eyes.

"I love you, Nora." The words he spoke were from his heart.

He waited for her to stiffen and pull away from him. He held his breath, listening to the pounding of his heart and the quickening of hers.

They'd worked their way across the dance floor into the corner shadows, and there Nora drew back, but only half a step. "I've never felt closer to anyone in my life, David." Her eyes were large and very serious. She looked away, out of the shadows and toward the musicians. They were still playing the same beautiful song.

She moved into his arms again. "I love you, too, David."

She drew a deep breath. The last strains of the music hung in the air. "I've been thinking it all day, but I didn't know that I'd be able to say it." The song ended, and with it the night drew to a close.

David was kissing her, and she was returning the kiss with all the passion and desire that had been locked up inside her and were now set free. He could still hear the music, but it was only in his head. The band had already put away their instruments.

When David and Nora finally broke apart, it was because the kiss had become too deep, too meaningful for it to continue there. They stood looking into each other's eyes, smiling their own secret smiles.

Somehow David managed to step away long enough to extract a roll of bills from his pocket, drop a few of them on the counter and others in a jar on the piano. The sax player and the pianist were talking quietly, but the man with the trombone still held it loosely in one hand before lifting it again to his lips and, with the mute in place, repeated the melody of that last familiar song. The strains followed them for more than a block, hauntingly beautiful.

Then, as if by design, a horse-drawn carriage let out a customer in front of a corner hotel. David flagged down the hansom and helped Nora into the seat. He slid in beside her and took her in his arms again.

Their kiss continued where it had left off in the club, a kiss of longing and unhidden desire. The music faded from Nora's head, to be replaced by a delicious dizziness that spun her around and around while his lips and teeth and tongue probed gently and then more demandingly. She was caught up in a passion unknown to her before. She couldn't hear the pounding of her heart, and she never did hear the voice that drifted back to them, its accent lilting and so familiar from her childhood.

David must have heard, but didn't respond until the voice repeated its request.

"'Scuse me, sir. You want me to go someplace or jus' set here?"

David drew his lips away from Nora's. "The Petite Auberge," he said before claiming her mouth again.

It was all a blur to Nora, the drive back through deserted streets to the hotel, David's hand on hers as she stepped from the carriage, his arm around her as they crossed the empty vestibule and walked down the hall to her room. She fumbled for the key, found it and tried to insert it in the lock. Her shaking hand prevented even that simple act.

David gently took the key from her and opened the door, and she marveled at his calmness, until he returned the key to her, placing it in the palm of her hand. His fingers, too, were trembling. It didn't matter now; nothing mattered now. They were in her room, and his arms were around her again.

Nora clung to David as if he were the beginning and the end of her world. There was nothing but David, his strong arms, his hard body, his fierce, burning kisses.

Piece by piece their clothes fell to the carpet, silently, as they were silent. Almost reverently David touched her hair, smoothing it beneath his hands. With deft fingers he removed the flower at her nape, brought it to his lips, inhaling the perfume before he let it drop to the floor. Then he began to take out the pins, one at a time, slowly. She didn't stir but let his fingers do their work until the last pin was removed and her hair, freed, tumbled to her shoulders. He buried his hands and then his face in its dark silkiness, breathing the fragrance, delighting in the texture, which was thick and smooth. After holding her at arm's length for a moment just to look, he reached out and took her hand in his.

The room was bathed in a half-light that gleamed on their bare arms, shoulders and backs as David led her to the bed. He watched as it shone on her hair and outlined the contours of her body, the curve of her chin and neck, collarbone and rising breasts, narrow waist and rounded hip.

"You're beautiful," he whispered. "Perfect." Just as he'd known she would be. His hands slid along her satiny-smooth skin, touching those beautiful curves that the light had outlined for him, feeling now what he'd only seen before.

Nora looked up at him, her throat tightening, her chest constricting with her need for him. His hand was at her breast. It was a light touch but a possessive one; it held her just as his eyes held her. Then his fingers began to caress the pink bud of her nipple. Deep inside she could feel the tension like a curling flame, growing. It caused her breath to quicken, her heart to pound.

Nora tried to put her feelings in words, but all she could muster was one faint word, his name. Then with a deep sigh she leaned against him.

"I know," he said. "I know." He kissed her and guided her gently to the bed beside him. "Let me love you, Nora. All I want is to love you." He'd managed to speak the words she'd tried to say just moments before, the words of need that had been so overpowering they'd caught on her lips. Again she tried; again her voice didn't come.

It didn't matter now as he closed her in his arms. She felt the texture of the hair on his chest, matted against her rising breasts. Somewhere deep within Nora heard the sultry, sexual tone of the trombone that had guided them as they'd left the club. It had found the notes to express desire, and it played for her now, in her head and in her heart. It was the music of love. She moved her hands to its sound as she traced the hard muscles of his back, the spare contours of his waist, the musculature of his thighs.

He kissed her until she thought she could stand the pleasure no longer, and then he took his mouth from hers and found her eager breast, and the pleasure was even greater than before. There was no music now, only the sound of her breathing, deep and jagged, accompanied by a little gasp. It came from far within her and caught on her lips as the words had caught there earlier.

He used his tongue to tease and tantalize her nipple until it was so taut and hard that she felt it would burst. Once more, just when she thought she could tolerate the pleasure no longer, he caught her turgid nipple between his teeth and bit gently, and the spirals of pleasure exploded within her and then all around as if to set off a celebration, their celebration of love.

Flashes of light and color were everywhere as his mouth found hers again, drinking from her lips, filling himself with her. He moved his tongue in and out of her eager mouth languorously, provocatively, foreshadowing the ultimate joining that was coming soon, so soon.

His fingers slid along her thigh, to her hip, down the curve of her abdomen. He rested the palm of his hand there for a moment, warm and strong, before slowly sliding his fingers lower until he found the moist sweetness that awaited him there. His tongue sought hers.

Nora was ready, eager, hungry for him. All this was new to her, this readiness that came so instantly when his lips touched her mouth or her breast or any part of her. He was ready, too, she found when she slid her hand between their damp bodies onto his waiting manhood, strong and swollen. She touched him and caressed him and loved him with her hand, duplicating the pleasure that he gave to her.

Their eagerness combined until they were both overcome by it. Neither could speak—they gasped for breath. Then for a moment they broke apart, their chests rising and falling in unison as they inhaled and tried to slow their racing hearts.

He was above her, looking down, ready but still waiting another moment to let the frenzy calm. With a gentle hand he pushed away her damp hair from her face. He kissed her eyelids, first one and then the other. He kissed the line of her nose, the angle of her cheekbone, the corner of her mouth.

With one hand still resting on her face, he rose above her and spoke softly, "I love you, Nora." With those words they were joined. They moved together as if they'd always been lovers, in perfect rhythm and harmony but at the same time with the joy of discovery and the wonder of newness.

It was wonder that David felt when she moved her hips to meet each of his languid strokes; it was wonder that caught him up in a frenzied passion and drove him on, faster and faster, until there was nothing left but a burning need that she answered, that ignited and set them both aflame.

GRADUALLY THEIR TUMULTUOUS HEARTS slowed and their breathing became easier. Pulling Nora into the cradle of his arms, David held her close. He was still caught up in her, lost in her loveliness and in the wonder of what had happened between them. He smoothed back her hair. The damp tendrils around her face had curled and added a girlish look to her beautiful face. He smiled to himself as he remembered removing the pins from her long hair and letting it cascade like a dark waterfall through his fingers. That was a moment he would never forget, a moment of such sensuality that his heart skipped a beat just thinking about it. The smile on his face had faded, and he was serious as he kissed her gently, sweetly. She was *his*, his Nora.

"This is what I've wanted from the beginning," he told her. "But at times I thought it would never happen."

Nora reached up to touch his face. Her fingers felt cool against his cheek. "You mean you doubted yourself?" Her words were teasing, but the question wasn't without some seriousness; he could tell from the look in her eyes.

He answered honestly. "I was unsure from the beginning, and the more I got to know you, the more I realized this was one time when I wouldn't be in control. Everything was up to you."

"Maybe it was always just a matter of time," she said.

"I think that's true. What happened tonight was inevitable."

Nora's fingers continued to stroke his face with a touch that was soft and languid. "I'm glad we waited. Thank you, David, for that."

"It wasn't easy," he admitted, "not from the very first moment I saw you."

Nora's fingers stopped their caressing. "You mean that night when I arrived—too late—at your apartment?"

"You weren't too late," he said, capturing her hand and kissing her fingertips. "You were just in time. At the opportune moment in my life, you walked through my door, cool and haughty."

"Not haughty, just professional," she corrected him.

"Okay," he agreed, "cool and professional with just a touch of haughtiness." He turned her slim hand in his and kissed her open palm. "At that moment, I decided I wanted you." He held her hand comfortably against his face. "And you decided you couldn't stand me. Am I right?"

"Well, I—"

"Come on, no secrets. Be honest."

"Well, I admit that I'd always thought you were somewhat overbearing on the telephone. Demanding..."

"Obnoxious?" he offered.

"If you say so."

"And what about the night we met, the night I fell instantly and forever in love? What were your feelings then?"

"I still didn't like you."

"Just as I thought. Not exactly love at first sight."

"Not exactly."

They were both quiet for a long moment before she said softly, "That came later."

At those words he gathered her up in his arms and held her close, not kissing her or even fondling her, just loving her as she loved him. "Why later?" he asked after a while. "What made you change?"

"I think it started happening when you told me about growing up, the dreams you had and your determination to make them come true. Then I saw your first project and knew there was something special about a man who could create such beauty."

"That was the beginning?"

"Yes," she said. "But it was this trip, being with you here in New Orleans, that proved how much you've come to mean to me, how important you are in my life. You came here because you thought I needed you, and I did. I needed you terribly." Her voice was shaky; she didn't try to control it.

"I want to be here for you, Nora. Will that be enough?" he asked, hoping he could live with her answer.

"I don't know, David. I can admit that I need you, but I've been on my own for a long time. I've always been in control...."

"I won't control you, Nora. I'll just be here, be close."

"Sometimes even that's hard for me."

"I know."

Her voice was firm now, no longer quavering. "Today when we were together, everything seemed so right. I felt so comfortable, as if we'd been a team for years."

"We are a team." He was caressing her again, kissing her all over, sending shivers up and down her spine. He could feel them under his hands. "Today seemed like a fantasy, the carriage ride, the dancing, even the afternoon by the river, but it wasn't make-believe, Nora. It was real, and when we get back to New York, it will continue just as it's been today. The city doesn't matter. We're all that matters." He cupped her breast with his hand, and her nipple grew taut beneath his touch. "Soon, very soon, you'll grow used to being close and loving me."

Her answer was in her eyes that looked into his, in her legs that twined with his and in her arms that slid around his neck as he covered her body with his own.

WHEN NORA AWOKE the room was bathed in sunlight. The curtains were open wide, and outside the patio and the little fountain sparkled with morning freshness. It was the beginning of another perfect day. She stretched on the rumpled sheets and smiled to herself. She could smell the scent of David all around her, and it made her head spin with delight. The pillow beside her was dented with the impression of his head. She looked around, expecting to see him, but the sunlit room was empty.

Then she saw the note on the bedside table.

You were sleeping so sweetly, I didn't want to waken you, although I couldn't resist a morning kiss. You said my name in your sleep. That was enough for me. I'll return soon. Don't, I repeat, *don't*, put your clothes back on!

Nora smiled. There wasn't much chance of that. Her dress and shawl lay in the middle of the floor, a wrinkled confusion of cotton and silk beneath a splash of red, the flower that had been tucked in her hair.

She swung her legs over the side of the bed and got up slowly, watching her reflection in the mirror, wondering if she'd changed and how she'd changed. She walked over to the mirror and examined herself closely. There were little love bites on her neck and breasts, her lips were pinkened and slightly swollen, but otherwise she was the same. Except for the glow. It was on her cheeks and it sparkled in her eyes. Yes, she *was* different. And she knew what the glow was. It was love.

She stood there in front of the mirror for a long time, staring at herself and thinking about what it meant to love David. It meant everything. It blotted out the world, her life, Keepsakes, even Phillip. Almost as important as the physical satisfaction she felt was the other, indescribable feeling that had come with their long talk afterward, the way he'd understood her thoughts and even her doubts.

Finally she moved away from the mirror and, taking her robe off the back of a chair, went into the bathroom. She turned on the shower and while it was running brushed the tangles from her hair and wrapped it on top of her head, securing it with a few pins. She'd already decided to wear it down today. He liked it that way.

After a long shower, Nora put on the terry-cloth robe and went back into the bedroom in time to hear a soft knock on the door. It opened, and David came in, carrying a white paper bag. "They tell me this is the best coffee in town. Chicory. I hope you like it."

"Indeed, I do," Nora answered. Nora had expected to feel shy seeing him again. Instead she felt completely at ease as he crossed the room and planted a kiss at the corner of her mouth.

"Or would you rather order breakfast from room service or go out to Brennan's?"

Nora shook her head. "Coffee is all I want. After that meal last night I'm not sure I'll ever be able to eat again." She accepted the cup of coffee, removed the lid and took a sip. "Umm, heavenly."

"You got dressed," he said with a mock pout.

"Just my robe." A little brazenly, she opened it enough for him to see that she was naked underneath.

"Good," he said huskily, reaching out to stroke the bare skin she'd revealed. After a long caress, he drew his hand away reluctantly, saying, "We have all morning." He looked at his watch. "Four hours, to be exact."

"You're leaving at noon?" Nora was surprised at the disappointment in her voice.

"Yes. I have a business meeting in New York tonight. I can't cancel it, Nora."

"I know, and I'm not asking you to. We were lucky to have these two days. They were so perfect, I just hate to see them end." Nora couldn't keep the sadness from her voice.

"The end for New Orleans," he said, "but just the beginning for us."

Nora sat down on the edge of the bed, sipping her coffee silently, her face a study in concentration.

"You don't seem to share my optimism," David said finally.

"You have to understand me, David. Everything in my life has been so transitory. Phillip's leaving, my mother's death. Even my childhood was taken from me."

"I understand that, Nora."

"My business is all I've had to hold on to, and even that . . . Well, look at it. I buy treasures for others to keep."

He stepped over to her, reaching down to put his hand on her shoulder. She rested her head against him. "You have me, and I'm not leaving you." She felt the fabric of his cotton trousers on her face. It was so personal, so intimate, resting her head against his hard, now familiar body, that she could almost believe in the permanence of him.

"I'll be in New York waiting for you. I won't walk away, Nora, and the more we're together, the more you'll believe in us and learn to trust me. I can promise you that."

When she didn't respond, he knelt down beside her, wrapping his arms around her waist, his head coming to rest on her breast. "We're magic, Nora. Everything's going to work out." Lightening the mood, he suggested, "Why don't we call now and get you on my plane?"

"I can't leave today, David. Business," she said weakly, and they both laughed. "I guess neither of us can shirk our responsibilities."

"Our clients should know what we're giving up," he said fervently. "What's on your schedule today?"

"Appointments with two antique dealers and some of Miss Lila's friends who want to show me their treasures."

"Will you see Lila again?"

"Oh, yes. I wouldn't want to cheat her out of a chance to talk about you."

"If she asks, tell her I'm a man with honorable intentions." His tone was teasing, but Nora realized he was serious.

"I know you are," she said.

He kissed her forcefully to allay any doubts. "Now," he said, sitting down beside her, "the next step is for me to meet Phillip and find out what he's all about. Maybe take some of that load off you."

"Phillip." Nora sighed. "I've hardly given him a thought. I feel terrible about that."

"Don't," David scolded. "You needed this time away."

"I just hope when I get back to New York, I'll know how to deal with that situation."

"You will, Nora. You're a marvelous combination of levelheadedness and sensitivity. How to handle Phillip, how to face his illness—that will all come to you. And I'll be there. Don't worry. I can help you take care of any problems."

When Nora's face still reflected doubt, David took her in his arms. Her robe slipped to the floor, and Nora forgot everything but David.

BECAUSE OF A FLIGHT DELAY, David spent an hour waiting at the New Orleans airport. While other passengers fretted all around him, David was relaxed. He had work to do on the flight, but he gave this unexpected time to introspection and thoughts of Nora.

The trip to New Orleans had been more successful than he could have imagined, and not only because he and Nora had become lovers. That was an added gift, one he hadn't dared to hope for. But there was so much more. Ever since their first meeting, he'd struggled long and hard to understand her, to learn what made her so damned independent sometimes and so needy other times. Now he knew, and that knowledge was the best gift.

It had come with the understanding of her background, her strange up-and-down childhood. Her once happy world had been torn away from her when Phillip's tenuous little empire had begun to crumble, again when he left and once more when Nora's mother died. David thought of his own childhood. To some, it might have seemed similar, but it wasn't. She'd lost everything—he'd lost nothing. There'd been nothing to lose.

Because he'd never known the luxury of a happy life in a beautiful world surrounded by belongings that represented his heritage, he'd never known what was missing. He could make his own rules, whereas Nora would forever play by a set of rules established through generations. A family, a background would continue to haunt her. He understood, and that understanding brought tears to his eyes.

David could almost visualize her as a child, her long dark hair in braids, sitting on the front steps of that magnificent old home in the Garden District. Hers had been a happy world until Phillip Chase had removed himself from it.

Whatever pain Phillip caused her in the future, David knew that he could help soothe it. Whatever problems he presented, David could help work them out. He made that promise to himself—and to Nora.

8

THE LAUGHTER RANG OUT over the tingling of fine crystal goblets clinked in a toast, of silverware on rare china, of flicking gold lighters held to the tips of expensive cigars. A few eyebrows were raised and a few pairs of eyes glanced toward David and his guest, Phillip Chase, and then glanced away. David was, after all, one of the club's most renowned members. His robust laughter would be overlooked.

In the cool and elegantly understated club, seated against dark paneled walls in deep arm chairs, feet resting on Persian wool, the club members went back to their conversations of business, politics and world affairs.

In David's corner of the room, the talk wasn't quite so lofty. In fact, a few times it had gotten downright bawdy as Phillip launched into tale after tale of fortunes won and lost over continents near and far. Most of it was farfetched, but David took it all with a grain of salt and enjoyed himself thoroughly.

"The world is full of women who are thanking their lucky stars that I never married them. As a lover I've had my moments, but as a husband, I was a total failure. Of course, I don't regret my one marriage for a moment—because of Nora."

It was the first mention of the woman who was their reason for being there, and in David's case, he thought suddenly, his reason for *being*. He let his mind drift away from Phillip to his daughter. She was still in New Orleans, and he could see her in his mind's eye, walking along rain-soaked streets on the way to an appointment, or lunching with Miss Lila amid all that bric-a-brac, or getting ready for bed in her room at the Petite Auberge. That memory stuck with him, and he lost himself in it. He could see her sitting before the mirror, removing the pins from her hair one by one and letting it tumble like a dark cloud to her soft shoulders.

When his thoughts of her began to get more provocative, David managed to push them away and concentrate on what Phillip was saying. Because he was talking about Nora, concentrating wasn't at all difficult.

"It's easy to see you're enamored of her," Phillip said.

David quirked an eyebrow in question, and Phillip laughed heartily. This time, none of the heads in the room turned toward them. David imagined that disappointed Phillip a little, the man obviously liked attention of whatever kind.

"Your eyes actually lit up when I mentioned her name, and I don't blame you one bit. She's a wonderful woman." He paused and lit a cigar. "I'm just glad she and I will be able to have this time together."

David heard the slight catch in Phillip's voice. The time would be limited for the father and daughter, and facing what the future had in store would be difficult for them both. Because David was concerned about how Nora was going to handle the time left, he'd called and arranged this meeting with Phillip Chase. He wanted to get to know him, possibly to find out something about the man that would help him understand the relationship between father and daughter and ultimately help Nora handle what lay ahead.

He'd tried to approach the meeting with no preconceived ideas, which had proved impossible. He'd brought Nora's feelings for her father with him, as mixed as those were. He could even admit now that he'd been prepared to dislike the man. To his surprise, David was both amused and charmed by Phillip Chase. His likability was of the surface variety, obviously, but David imagined that even Phillip would admit that, and when he talked about his daughter, the love in his voice was genuine. For all else he might be, Phillip Chase was terribly fond of Nora. And yet he'd hurt her desperately.

"It was a surprise for her, your turning up again after so many years," David said. He didn't want to sound as if he were interrogating Phillip, but he had to at least make that observation in order to get a response.

"I know what you're thinking," Phillip said as he took a sip of his brandy and lingered over the taste. "You're thinking I stayed away too long. Well, I did, but when you get right down to it, David, she was probably better off without me."

David had to agree, silently at least, with that.

"For a few years after I left, my luck was pretty bad, and I was just as glad that she and her mother weren't there to see it." He drank some more brandy and followed it with a puff on the ever-present cigar. "Yes, I missed the boat with a few of my schemes. Hell, once or twice the boat sailed away while I was waiting at the airport!" He laughed again, this time at his own misfortune. "I hit pay dirt a few times after that. Living abroad was good for me, but I'm glad to be back with Nora. She's special."

"I know," David agreed, "and I couldn't bear to see her hurt again. Not by anyone." He met Phillip's eyes evenly and with a smile that took some of the edge off his words.

Smile or not, Phillip was perturbed. "You're sounding rather proprietary."

David had the grace to laugh. "I guess I am, but that's the way I feel toward her."

"Nora is very independent."

David felt irritation cut through him. Phillip hadn't seen his daughter in years, yet he had the audacity to tell David what she was all about. David's voice revealed his reaction. "I know all about her independence and her intelligence. She's also very resilient." He waited to let that sink in. It was the resilience that had helped her to get through those years without a father, and Phillip knew that very well. "She's also vulnerable," David added. "That may not be obvious to everyone."

"No," Phillip agreed, "just to those of us who love her."

For a moment David was put off-balance, reminded that he wasn't the only one who loved Nora Chase. He started to respond, but Phillip was smiling, a smile that David had to admit was disarmingly candid.

"Our roles seem to be reversed, David. Shouldn't the father be lecturing the suitor, not vice versa?"

The remark brought an answering smile to David's lips and a return to camaraderie between the two men.

David lifted his glass in a salute. "You're right, Phillip. I've been lecturing you. I guess you have to put it down to my feelings for your daughter."

"I'll be glad to do so. I'm touched that you love Nora."

It was a statement, but David answered as if it had been a question. "Yes," he said, "I love her." He said it because he wanted to say it. It felt good, felt right to declare his love. When he had first told Nora he loved her, that had been special for him, and for her, he believed, but there was power now in saying it out loud to someone else. "I love her," he repeated softly, wishing she were there so he could say the words to her again.

"I couldn't be happier," Phillip declared. "I've heard all about you, of course."

David looked at the older man with surprise.

"Oh, not from Nora. She hasn't opened up to me yet, hasn't let me in to any of the private places. I hope she will eventually."

David sensed that he meant what he said. Nora's father had sorely missed her.

"Janice has talked about you," Phillip added with a grin. "She talks about everyone. And everything. A delightful child, but she never stops."

David laughed. "That's true, but I'll be forever in her debt. She was a great help in my pursuit of Nora."

"I can well imagine," Phillip said. "She's obviously a big fan of yours. She told me everything about *the* David Sommer. I wasn't exactly uninitiated myself, however. I've seen some of your work abroad."

"Really?" This was the opening he'd been waiting for, the chance to hear about Phillip's recent sojourn in Europe. Phillip was certain to drop some very important names—that was his style. Among the names, there might be one or two of David's acquaintance. That's all he'd needed. He sat back, relaxed in the red leather armchair, and waited.

"Yes," Phillip said, squinting against the smoke that curled up around him. "I'm particularly fond of the building you codesigned with Jean-Paul deValet in Monaco."

"So you know Jean-Paul?" He wondered if this could be the connection.

"Not personally," Phillip replied. David would have to wait for a few more names to crop up. "I know his work and have always admired it. There's something lilting about his buildings."

David agreed. "He's a very poetic designer."

A second glass of brandy had made Phillip mellow, a little more thoughtful and less talkative. The other patrons of the club must have appreciated that, but David was anxious to get back to the stories.

He didn't have to wait long.

"Actually," Phillip said, "I have met Jean-Paul, only casually, of course. I'm sure he wouldn't remember me," he added a little modestly.

David didn't share that sentiment. He expected that everyone who'd met Phillip Chase, heard at least a few of his tales, been around him long enough to get charmed or conned or both, would remember.

Phillip was jogging his memory and coming up with more names. "I believe we attended a dinner party together at the home of the Comte and Comtesse Beaucaire. They have a summer house in Brittany."

David smiled. "Yes, I believe I've met them. Didn't their daughter marry an American film actor? What was his name?" David pretended a lapse of memory, and Phillip stepped in. He had an amusing anecdote about the actor, which led to more Beaucaire family stories. As he listened, David relaxed and let himself be entertained. He had what he wanted.

"You seem to know everyone," David ventured amid Phillip's new batch of reminiscences.

Phillip shrugged. "I've lived abroad for a long time. It suits my life-style. I should think it would suit yours, as well," he commented, misjudging, as people often did, David's tastes. That he wasn't the bon vivant he was made out to be was known only to his closest friends. And to Nora.

"In fact," Phillip continued, "I'm surprised you don't work more in Europe. Aren't you interested in designing homes such as the Beaucaires'?"

"Certainly, if the opportunity is right. It depends on circumstances." Suddenly David realized that Phillip had something in mind. David couldn't resist a smile. They'd been leading each other on, both going in the same direction for different purposes. No wonder this had all been so easy. They were playing the same game!

"As you've gathered, I have many good friends over there."

David nodded. It was coming now.

"Among them, I'm sure there would be many opportunities that would appeal to you." Phillip seemed to be mulling this over, but David had a feeling he'd already settled on just the opportunity. "For example," he said offhandedly, "I happen to know a family of the French aristocracy."

David nodded knowingly.

"They own property along the waterfront at Biarritz, a long stretch that is, amazingly, not developed. I expect they've just been waiting for the right time, and I'm told that time is just about upon them." Phillip grinned conspiratorially. "They've lived somewhat above their means, and money is getting low. You know how it is among the aristocracy." He didn't wait for an answer, assuming that David was with him all the way. "They might be persuaded to consider the right kind of development, in good taste, of course, to protect the family's image."

"Hmm," David said noncommittally.

"Maybe if I gave this some more thought, made a few inquiries . . . Of course, I wouldn't contact the family directly unless you were really interested in the project."

"Of course," David agreed. "What sort of agreement were you thinking about?"

"Between whom?" Phillip asked, full of naiveté.

"Why, between you and me, of course, Phillip."

"Well, I . . ."

Suddenly both men started to laugh, more loudly than before, but now they were virtually alone in the room, so their laughter rang out over the elegant but empty tables.

"You're on to me," Phillip said finally.

"Let's just say I get the picture, Phillip."

"Well, does it sound like a good deal or not?"

"It has fascinating possibilities."

"Then what about a fifteen percent finder's fee?"

"I believe five is customary."

"Ten?"

"Eight," David said.

"Done."

"That is," David reminded Phillip, "if and when this project ever gets off the ground. That's a big *if* and an equally big *when*."

"Granted," Phillip answered, sitting back and lighting another cigar. He looked to David like a man who had no doubts about the certainty of his idea coming to fruition. "Shall I start making inquiries?"

"I don't think so, Phillip. I'll need to do some research first. I'll let you know as soon as I make a decision to move ahead. As I said, it could take some time."

"I'll wait," Phillip assured his younger friend.

DAVID SAT at his drawing board the next morning, working on a new project but unable to give it the effort it needed. Finally he put the drafting materials aside and leaned back in his chair, and found himself chuckling aloud. The sound brought his new secretary to the door. Tentatively, she poked her head through.

"Is everything all right, Mr. Sommer?"

"Yes, everything's fine. I'm just laughing at myself."

"Oh, I see," she said, disappearing.

She didn't see at all, David thought, wishing that Maggie were still with him and not traipsing around Peru. He'd enjoy telling Maggie about the scene last night with Phillip Chase. She'd get a kick out of the two men trying to outdo each other. In a way, they'd both achieved their objectives.

David already had an assistant looking into the possibilities of the Biarritz property. The project could be interesting, to develop a waterfront area in an overcrowded tourist town in a way that wouldn't spoil the environment. A real challenge. Of course, Phillip would get his eight percent, his objective achieved, an unusual one for a man at death's door, David thought. But, then, Phillip was an unusual man. Maybe even the threat of imminent death couldn't quell his gambling spirit.

As for David, he'd come out of the meeting with more than a prospective new project. He'd been looking for a contact, a close friend who was also on intimate terms with Phillip. He'd found one: Comte Beaucaire, "Charles" to his friends.

As he buzzed his secretary to put in a long distance call to Charles Beaucaire in Paris, David thought over what he was about to do. At its best, it was inquisitiveness, at its worst, spying. But David felt justified.

He needed to know more about Phillip Chase, a charmer without doubt, an amusing and interesting man who put even David under his spell, but a hard man to get a handle on. For Nora's sake, he needed to find out what Phillip was all about. He had a sneaking suspicion he knew the answer. He hoped he was wrong.

NORA THOUGHT SHE'D NEVER get away from New Orleans. Lila had lined up not three but four appointments for her. Within Lila's large circle of friends, parting with an occasional heirloom in order to pick up a little pin money had become a kind of sport for the ladies, a fascinating game. Would it be Sophie's filigree earrings or Emmaline's diamond brooch? The possibilities were unlimited, and as teatime turned into sherry time in New Orleans, they became the topic of conversation.

Nora had gone through all this before. She often received calls in New York from one of the group with an item to offer Keepsakes. She'd been hard-pressed to explain that she did *not* own an antique shop and had nowhere to store the proffered sets of china, hand-painted vases and collections of miniatures. They hadn't listened then and still weren't listening, so Nora found herself visiting in the homes of wealthy or once wealthy ladies, most of them widows or single older women, all of them bent on achieving a coup by making a sale to Keepsakes, whether they needed the money or not.

Politely Nora made lists of all the valuables for future reference, explaining that as soon as she found an interested client, she would certainly be in touch. Lila was beside herself, because the only item Nora actually went away with was her tea set. Not only would the money keep her going for a while, Lila argued, but the prestige would be invaluable.

Throughout the long day, Nora had tried valiantly but with little success to keep her mind on business. She kept drifting away in the midst of the scent of lavender and the taste of mint to other sensations, all of them physical, all of them connected to David.

Finally she was back in New York, in a taxi heading for her apartment. Almost forty-eight hours had passed since she'd seen David, but not a moment had passed that she hadn't thought about him. He had a business trip planned for the next day, and Nora wanted to hear his voice before he left. She glanced at the watch on her lapel. It was late but still not too late to call. Suddenly she felt shy, wondering if she'd be able to say what was on her mind, how much she'd missed him and wanted him, how much she loved him. Nora was still forming words for a conversation with David when she let herself into her apartment.

There were lights on in the living room, not just the desk lamp that Janice usually left on for her, but all the lights. There was music playing, too, Chopin in the stereo, and in the air the scent of an expensive cigar.

"Damn," she said softly to herself as she dropped her suitcase in the hall and placed the boxed tea set carefully beside it. She'd counted on Phillip being in his room. Her thoughts were still confused about him, her mother, the past. She hadn't had time to process everything that Lila had told her, especially the nagging suspicion that she may have misjudged him, that her interpretation of what had happened when she was sixteen years old had been somehow colored by her mother's views. All that was possible, but Nora couldn't face those possibilities now.

"Nora?" Her father's voice called out from the living room.

He'd always been a night owl. She should have known he wouldn't go off to bed tonight of all nights. Suppressing a sigh, Nora stepped through the doorway.

He rushed to greet her. "Welcome home, my dear." Phillip placed a kiss on both cheeks, European-style, and then stepped back to look at her. "How lovely you are."

Nora suspected that she looked as bedraggled as she felt, but Phillip, on the other hand, was in fine fettle, bright-eyed, sporting a cravat tucked into the neck of his silk dressing gown and smelling of expensive cologne. "I decided to wait up for you."

"That wasn't necessary," Nora managed, her tone only barely civil.

"Of course it wasn't, but I wanted to. Now come in and tell me all about the trip, about New Orleans and Lila."

Nora allowed herself to be drawn into the room and pulled down on the sofa beside Phillip, after which she gave him a brief account of her visit. She didn't mention David. There was no need to, and she wasn't ready to talk about him. What she and David had was too personal and intimate to share, especially with her father, whom she barely knew. Maybe someday she would be able to talk about her relationship with David, but not yet. Playing father had only recently become Phillip's role, and she wasn't prepared to sit still for advice, which he was sure to offer.

But Nora did get caught up in telling him about New Orleans. Egged on, she began to enjoy herself thoroughly. Soon they were discussing changes in the French Quarter, the lack of changes among the old families in the Garden District, the new menu at Nettie and André's and the chef's predictable weight gain, all of which Nora related in detail.

"I expect Lila's her old self, too," Phillip commented after he'd listened attentively to the stories. "Arranging get-togethers, running up bills and gossiping."

"I don't suppose she'll ever change."

"We wouldn't want her to."

"No, we wouldn't," she agreed. There was no excluding the strong bond of their shared memories. It felt good.

"Now what about the tea set? You brought it back I expect?"

"Oh, yes. Not without some difficulty, though. I was so petrified that it would be broken," she admitted, "that I held it like a baby on the plane."

"Did she make a good deal?"

Nora laughed. "Let's say we were both satisfied." For some reason she hesitated to bring her father into the details of her business arrangement.

"Well, whatever the price," he said, ignoring her hesitation, "your client will get her tea set. I'm pleased. And I think you'll be pleased to know that I've been busy, too."

"Oh?" Nora was anxious to say good-night now, go to her room and call David. She'd been drawn into a conversation that had turned out to be quite delightful, but enough was enough.

"Oh, yes," Phillip went on, "I found something very suitable for Dr. Irving—"

Nora couldn't help responding to that. "He hasn't called in a long time."

"Well, I guess he's come back to the fold. Actually, I found his card in the file and gave *him* a call. I thought the time might be right—"

"You what?" Nora was astounded that her father had gone through her files.

"Yes, I judged correctly," he said, misinterpreting her astonishment. "Just sixth sense, I guess, but the doctor seemed about at that age when the eye begins to roam. And as I suspected, there's a new lady in his life. He wanted a gift for her birthday. I gather that he's something of a man of the world."

"He's an old reprobate," Nora corrected, still steaming about her father's invasion of the business files.

Phillip paid no attention. "He was very pleased with the gift I chose—and paid handsomely for it, I might add. I'm sure you'll agree that I earned myself a tidy little commission."

Nora's anger went off in every direction at Phillip's presumption. Unable to decide where to center her anger, she chose to be guided by common sense. She'd nod politely, say good-night and deal with this in the morning.

Phillip didn't give her the chance. He was determined to tell all. "I decided on a fifty-percent markup with a twenty-five percent commission." Finally he caught the look on his daughter's face and added hastily, "Of course, I plan to share the profits with you."

That did it. Nora's anger blazed in her eyes and in her cheeks. Phillip was acting as if he owned Keepsakes, offering to give her a share of profits in her own business, which he'd insinuated himself into without any previous agreement. Well, she would have to deal with this here and now—it couldn't be put off until tomorrow.

Trying to keep the shakiness from her voice, Nora said, "There is nothing I can do about what happened while I was gone, but I intend to make myself very clear about the future. This business is mine. I started it. I made it successful. Much of that success is due to the rapport I've built up with my clients, and I don't want anything to interfere with that, including my own father."

"You're upset over nothing, Nora," Phillip answered soothingly. "The doctor was very pleased with his gift."

"The doctor is hardly the point, Phillip. When I'm not here, Janice is in charge, and Janice answers to me."

Her voice did have a tremor in it, and Nora hated herself for it.

"Janice and I talked this over," he retorted, "and she agreed with me—"

"Before you talked to Dr. Irving or after?" Nora asked curtly.

"Well, afterward, I'll admit, but Janice was very enthusiastic. He'd been a difficult client to win over, and it seems I was successful." Realizing that he was bragging, Phillip changed his tactics. "You're getting needlessly upset, Nora." He spoke calmly, patronizing her, placating her as if she were a child.

Nora answered sharply. "I agreed for you to live here with me, Phillip, because I want to be as much help as I can during your illness, but I don't remember discussing your becoming part of Keepsakes."

"I only wanted to help you out, my dear." He seemed genuinely confused by her anger.

Unable to sit still any longer, Nora got up from the sofa to move around the room. "This isn't the way to help, Phillip. My clients are important to me. I need to deal with them just as I always have." The thought crossed Nora's mind that she was being irrational, but she ignored it. No one had given Phillip permission to interfere in Keepsakes. His mere presence in her home was difficult enough for her to deal with. He'd invaded her personal life, now he was moving in on her professionally. She couldn't cope with that

"You've done a wonderful job, Nora, and that's why I think the party I've planned for Saturday is a good idea."

"Party?" Nora couldn't believe her ears—this was getting totally out of hand.

"It's for your grateful clients, Nora. You must admit I've always been an outstanding host. I hope you'll approve this time."

Nora's rage was almost uncontrollable as she began to realize the extent of Phillip's interference, not just in her work but in her life. "How dare you, Phillip. How dare you come back into my life and expect me to pick up where we left off? No," she corrected. "Not even where we left off."

Nora was seeing red. "You're pretending that over the years you've been a loving father, and you're expecting me to welcome you back. Well, you weren't, and I can't," she declared. "You left me Phillip, and I'll never forgive you. If you weren't dying, I wouldn't have you here. Do you understand?" She hadn't meant to say that, but it was too late. She'd lost control.

Through her rage, Nora saw the look on his face. It was one of sadness, disappointment and deep regret. He seemed to age before her eyes. He dropped the cigar he was smoking into the ashtray and leaned back on the sofa. "I'm sorry, Nora," he said. "I'm just an old fool to think that I could make it up to you this way. I guess I've failed you again."

"I—" Nora stopped, not sure what she'd meant to say.

"Don't worry, I'll cancel the party plans. There's nothing I can do about Dr. Irving, but I certainly won't contact any of your other clients. I made a mistake, but it was because I wanted to help, not to hurt. Please believe that. You're my daughter, my little girl, the only one I'll ever have."

It was as if something inside Nora gave way, like a dam breaking. He was her father, whom she'd once loved beyond imagining. She could feel the sadness and terrible pain for all the years that had been wasted. It flowed through her and washed the anger away with its power, freeing her from the bonds of the past and leaving her cleansed.

As if Phillip couldn't bear to see the released emotions in his daughter, he looked away. "Whatever you believe about me, Nora, I want you to know that I love you. Is there anything more important than love?"

"No," she answered as her eyes filled with the tears that were breaking through at last.

Phillip stood up and opened his arms to her. "Come here," he said, "come to your dad, Nora."

The tears cascaded down her cheeks then, freeing tears that washed away all the years of sadness. "Oh, Daddy," she said, "I'm so glad you're here."

His arms closed around her, and Nora laughed and cried at the same time, her pain mixed with newfound joy. "Let's go ahead with your plans for Saturday night," she said with sudden enthusiasm. "More than anything I want to celebrate."

"Do you think I still have my touch?" Phillip asked, his voice still shaky with emotion.

"There's not the slightest doubt in my mind. We'll show New York what a real party's like."

THE BUXOM MRS. BISHOP, wearing the brooch Phillip had chosen for her, had him cornered between the sofa and a large potted plant, while Phillip's gaze kept drifting toward Dr. Irving's new girlfriend. Janice saw Phillip's predicament but couldn't help him out. She, too, was trapped by not one but two clients.

Nora missed both these encounters because David had arrived. For an unprofessionally long time, she had eyes for no one else. He'd managed to move her away from the activity to a relatively quiet part of the living room, dodging the hired butler and his tray of hors d'oeuvres.

"Wouldn't you like a drink?" Nora asked. A bar had been set up in the dining room.

"Not even slightly," David responded. He couldn't take his eyes off Nora, who was dressed in a gown of flame-red chiffon. "I'm trying to regain my senses, but you're making it difficult." David took a deep breath and managed to look away from her around the room. "This is some party. I have a feeling it's more than just a Keepsakes celebration."

"Yes," Nora admitted. "Phillip and I have come to an understanding. I guess you could call this a celebration of our reunion." She looked up at David with a radiant smile, and his heart caught. Never had she looked more beautiful.

"We had a terrible scene the night I came home from New Orleans," she went on. "I was so angry with him—I even hated him for a moment. Then I realized that I hated him because he'd hurt me so and that he couldn't hurt me if I didn't love him."

"You've forgiven him?" David felt a twinge of nervousness, wondering whether he should tell her his suspicions about Phillip. He hadn't been able to reach Charles yet, but he'd left a message. Soon he'd know a lot more about Nora's father. He couldn't shake off the feeling that Phillip was a charlatan and that regardless of his good intentions, he could hurt Nora again.

"I haven't forgiven him, really. I've just tried to forget. Oh, we've had a wonderful talk, all about him and Mother and why he left New Orleans. He wanted her to come with him, but she wouldn't. I never knew that. He realized there was no future for him in New Orleans—he had to leave, David. Mother had to stay. It was all predestined in a way. He really didn't desert us."

Her face was so full of life and hope and love that David couldn't say any more. Instead he leaned down and kissed her cheek. "I've missed you, Nora. It's only been a few days, but they've been hell for me. I wanted you so much—I want you right now," he declared, ignoring the crowds around them. "Can't we slip away together and leave your father to handle the party?"

His lips drifted quickly along the curve of her neck, breathing the heady scent of her perfume and hearing the whisper of her breath. He'd never seen her in red before. She usually wore cool, muted colors, but tonight she looked exotic and enticing in her bright dress and bright lipstick. Her hair was pinned up, but with a high-fashion sweep that was maddeningly provocative. As beautiful as it was, he wanted to disturb the sweep with his hands, bury them in her dark hair and loosen the strands until they fell to her shoulders, just like that night in New Orleans. Then he wanted to slip the bright red dress off and hold her close to him again.

She turned and kissed him, a fleeting but tantalizing kiss on the lips. "We can't leave now, but don't give up hope," she teased. The muscle in David's cheek twitched as he gritted his teeth and tried to get control of himself. She took his hand. "Right now I want you to come and talk to Phillip—to my father," she corrected. "He's really quite charming, David, once you get to know him." She looked up at him with her large dark eyes, which had the power to melt his heart. "You'll like him. I know you will."

"Of course I will. He's your father," David answered simply. He'd decided not to mention his dinner with Phillip. Obviously Phillip hadn't told her about it, and it didn't matter now, not when Nora was so happy, glowing like a bright flame. Maybe he could put that disturbing encounter out of his mind and begin afresh tonight. Maybe Charles wouldn't return his call, and he could forget about Phillip's past, go ahead innocently toward the future, as Nora had chosen to do. Perhaps that would be best for them all.

9

TO CALL THE CROWDED ROOM that Nora and Phillip rummaged through an antique shop would be an undeserved compliment. It was a junk store, but an imaginative one. While Phillip chatted with the owner, Nora prowled around in back, trying without much success to avoid cobwebs and dust. A sooty fifteen minutes into her search, she called out, "Phillip, come and look. I think I've found something."

More fastidious than his daughter, Phillip threaded his way carefully to the back of the store. "What in the world is it?" He looked at the large wooden object with its peeling paint. "A totem pole?"

She was about to scold, when she saw the teasing gleam in his eye. "You know exactly what this is. It's a figurehead from an old sailing ship, the perfect gift for Mrs. Sullivan's husband. She wanted something special for his fiftieth birthday."

"He sails," Phillip recalled.

"They have a beach house."

"This may be the solution." Phillip helped Nora pull the figurehead from where it was wedged between two unidentifiable objects. "Should we have it repainted?"

"I don't think so. This is the original paint," Nora said, examining her find closely.

"It needs restoring, though."

Nora looked up at her father. "Couldn't you do that?"

"Yes, I think I could."

"Then let's take it." Nora started to drag the huge carving toward the front of the store.

"Maybe we should call Mrs. Sullivan first, just to be sure."

"Oh, come on, Phillip," she teased. "Live dangerously." Phillip laughed. His daughter was throwing his own philosophy back at him.

Somehow they managed to get themselves and the figurehead into a taxi, exhausted as much by their laughter as their struggle.

"I think she looks quite provocative, hanging out the window like that," Phillip observed after giving the driver Nora's address. The carving of a woman with hair that had once been bright red but was now faded to pink jutted out in Nora's side, her enormous breasts residing on Nora's lap. "Maybe we should change places," he commented wickedly.

"Never," Nora said. "I'm incapable of moving even for a good effect. When we get home, the driver will have to pull her out through the window. I suppose we'll gather quite a crowd of sightseers." She squirmed to get more comfortable and pulled her collar more tightly around her neck.

A brisk breeze blew through the window, bringing with it the sharp scents of autumn. Nora took a deep breath. The air was heady and invigorating, and she gloried in the change of seasons. Everything seemed more vibrant to her now. All her senses were heightened, and she appreciated more fully the everyday occurrences of life that she had once taken for granted.

Part of the change in her was due to Phillip. Because of his illness, she'd learned to savor each moment they shared and to try to push away the anxieties about his health. Today he seemed well; that was all that really counted, and for that she gave thanks.

Both Phillip *and* David had transformed her life these past few weeks. David. She thought about him and closed her eyes. He'd been traveling again, but she'd see him tonight and was looking forward to their date as eagerly as a teenager. They would laugh and talk, and then he'd hold her and she'd find comfort in the strength of his arms. For the first time she believed in the power of love to change lives.

The cab pulled up to her apartment, where Phillip, ignoring Nora's objections, helped the cabdriver unload the figurehead, egged on by a vocal crowd of onlookers. Nora stumbled out, offering the driver an extra tip to carry the huge wooden object up to her apartment.

"No such thing," her father said, paying the driver and sending him on his way. "I can handle this."

"Do you think you should?" Nora asked, concerned about Phillip's overexerting himself. But it was too late. He'd already heaved the figurehead onto his shoulder and was heading across the lobby to the elevator. With a shrug, Nora followed.

Finally the three of them were standing solemnly in the elevator, similar quixotic smiles on all three faces.

"Push the button," Nora ordered as one of the building's tenants approached.

"Not a chance," Phillip replied. "Keep your wooden smile. I want to see the reaction."

The tenant, an obese woman wearing a bulky fur coat, stepped onto the elevator, looked from one expressionless face to the other and quickly stepped off again. Phillip pushed the button and the doors slid closed, but not before two of the three burst out laughing.

Janice must have heard the laughter all the way down the hall, for she was in the doorway waiting. She looked askance at the carving. "You two are going to give the neighborhood a bad name."

"We three," Phillip corrected.

"Yes," Nora agreed. "Phillip, Gertrude and I."

"Gertrude?" Janice repeated.

"She looks like Gertrude to me. Phillip?"

"No," he joked, "not Phillip, definitely Gertrude." Once more he and his daughter broke up.

"Have you been drinking?" Janice wondered as she stepped aside to let them pass.

"We're drunk on autumn. It's glorious out there."

"I wish I could get out to see for myself," Janice complained, adding to Phillip, "please put it in the living room. There's enough confusion in the office. I've never been so busy," she told Nora. "The phones are ringing off the hooks."

"A direct result of the party," Phillip said proudly, stashing the figurehead in a corner of the dining room.

"There's no doubt about that," Nora agreed. She waited for her father and let him take her coat. "You should be very proud."

"Thank you, my dear," he answered with an exaggerated bow. "But I'm a little fatigued from the morning's expedition. I think I'll lie down, while you girls—" he added as the phones began to ring "—look to your business."

After they'd handled their calls, Nora took both phones off the hook, put on her tortoiseshell glasses and started going through the messages that were piled high on her desk. "This is ridiculous," she said almost immediately. "Did everyone in Manhattan call?"

"Almost everyone," Janice answered. "I never knew there could be so many anniversaries, birthdays, baby showers. It's unreal."

"We'll just have to wade through, hoping not to drown."

"Phillip can save us, especially since many of the calls are for him. Your father's gathered quite a coterie of ladies who want him to pick out their gifts personally."

"No one has ever denied Phillip's charm," Nora affirmed.

"Even you?" Janice asked slyly.

"Especially me. I couldn't be more pleased about our relationship. We're making up for all the lost years."

"At the same time, everything's going great with you and David," Janice reminded her.

Nora didn't need to be reminded. Her friend was only voicing Nora's earlier thoughts. "I just hope all this happiness doesn't suddenly go up in smoke." She looked at Janice with a serious expression. "Maybe it's more than I deserve."

"Don't be silly," Janice scolded. "You deserve it all. And so do I, for that matter."

Nora leaned back thoughtfully in her chair. "The only cloud on the horizon is Phillip's health."

Janice nodded solemnly. "What's the latest medical report?"

"Still in remission, according to Phillip."

"But you haven't talked to the doctor."

"No. Phillip is adamant about that. He insists that he's a grown man and can take care of himself. I haven't had the nerve to interfere, but as soon as I see a sign that he's not doing well—anything at all—I'm going to call the doctor. I know Phillip will be angry, but I don't care, Janice. I'm his daughter," she said firmly—and proudly.

NORA'S EUPHORIA accompanied her to David's that night, but she left behind all doubt that she deserved her happiness. She deserved every bit of it, especially David's love. They were good for each other.

He'd offered to cook dinner for her, and she arrived with a bottle of wine and a dozen roses. Aware that this might be considered a reversal of roles by some, Nora didn't care in the least. She was a terrible cook. The wine and roses were all she had to offer. Well, not quite all. She had her love, which David seemed to think was enough.

Getting no answer to her knock, Nora turned the knob, and swung open the door.

"David?"

"I'm out in the kitchen," came the answer, causing Nora to smile. This really was a reversal.

A marvelous aroma drifted toward her, and Nora headed for the kitchen. She was intercepted by David. "No fair peeking," he said as he grabbed her and kissed her hungrily, squashing the roses. "The sauce needs time to simmer, alone and undisturbed...."

"Sauce?" Nora managed to deposit her gifts on the table without leaving David's arms.

"Yep. Just like Mom used to make. We're having spaghetti, but it's about two hours away from perfection." He planted a kiss on her neck. "I see you brought flowers. You're the perfect date," he added with a laugh.

"And wine," she murmured, luxuriating in the feeling of his strong body as he held her close. "I'll need a vase and a corkscrew." She moved again toward the kitchen.

"Oh, no, you don't." He let her go reluctantly and made a quick trip to the kitchen, returning with all the necessary accoutrements—a vase filled with water, a corkscrew and two wineglasses.

Nora arranged the flowers while David poured the wine, both of them exchanging kisses along with their duties. Handing her a glass of wine, he smiled and said, "You look like you've had a good day."

"It's been perfect. Phillip and I went antiquing and enjoyed ourselves thoroughly. It's great fun being a daughter again."

David turned away to recork the wine and also to avoid looking directly at Nora.

Still euphoric, Nora was unaware of the frown that played across his features. "It's fun working with Phillip, too. As you saw at the party, he has a way with customers."

"He certainly does," David was able to agree, but without adding anything else to Nora's description of her father. He left that to her, and she obliged readily.

"I'm beginning to understand him at last, David. Somehow I don't think my mother ever did."

"That's because they saw life differently, Nora."

"I know. He couldn't resist challenges, adventures. She needed safety and security. I think she knew that, too." Nora sighed deeply. "Unfortunately they fell in love, and there wasn't anything they could do about that. I think they always loved each other. I know neither of them ever loved anyone else. It just wasn't meant to be."

David turned to Nora and looked at her tenderly. "*This* is meant to be, though, Nora." He reached out and touched her face. "Our love. We were meant to be together, not apart."

"But we've been apart so much," Nora reminded him.

"I know, and I'm putting a stop to all that. No more business trips for a while. I'm designating the travel to my associates, and I'm staying right here in New York. As for you," he added, kissing the corner of her mouth, "if anyone needs a keepsake that can't be found in New York—"

"I'll send Janice," Nora finished for him.

"Exactly." He kissed the tip of her nose. "And speaking of gifts, I have one for you."

"It's not my birthday."

David laughed. "No, it isn't. It's also not Christmas or Valentine's Day, but an occasion isn't always necessary. Haven't your customers ever told you that?"

"I guess so," Nora said almost shyly.

"But no one has ever bought you a present without a reason?"

Nora shook her head.

"Then this is a first. Wait a minute. I'll be right back."

When David returned with a brightly wrapped box, he corrected his earlier remark. "There *is* a reason." He handed her the box. "It's because I love you. That'll always be reason enough for me."

Nora pulled off the ribbons and wrapping paper, opened the box and unfolded the layers of tissue to reveal a splash of brilliant red filmy material. She held it up, enchanted.

"David," she whispered. "I've never had a nightgown so . . ."

"Sexy?"

She nodded.

"I thought so. Your clothes are beautiful, but I was beginning to think you wore only muted soft colors until I saw you at the party in that red dress. You really knocked me out. So I thought—" his voice became husky with unspoken needs "—you might wear this just for me."

She held the silky material against her face and looked at him from under lowered lids. "Of course, I'll wear it for you."

"Now?"

"I'll need to get undressed."

He looked sharply at her. There was an innocent smile on her face but an impish shine in her eyes.

"That can be arranged," he said.

"I might need some help."

"Yes, I thought you might." David stood up, and with one easy motion lifted Nora into his arms. "I believe it's time you were introduced to my bedroom."

In a few long strides he was across the floor and moving down the hall. He kicked open the door to his bedroom and turned on the light. If Nora had been aware of her surroundings at that moment, she would have noticed a room designed to David's specifications, L-shaped with thick carpets and draperies and modern but comfortable furniture. But Nora wasn't aware of David's room, only of David.

And David, too, saw nothing except the woman in his arms. He'd flung the nightgown over his shoulder, and as he put her down he let his fingers slide across it, while one arm still held her firmly. He could feel the pounding of his heart and the drumming of his blood. He was on fire for her and wanted nothing more than to make love to her.

But he stopped himself. First he had to see her in the gown, fulfill the fantasy he'd had when he'd bought it, his fantasy of Nora wearing the flimsy scarlet gown. Yet he wasn't sure he'd be able to wait, because she was standing on tiptoe and kissing him, softly but eagerly, again and again. His lips parted, and her tongue sneaked deliciously into his mouth.

David felt his head swim, and although he tried to step back so he could help her undress, he couldn't keep his hands from roaming over her, drifting through her long hair, down her back, cupping her firm buttocks, drawing her closer and closer. He knew that unless he got control of himself, his hands would be ripping at her clothes, and together they would tumble onto the bed, where it would be over much too soon.

Controlling his hands at last, he placed them on her shoulders and forced himself to move back half a step. He fumbled with the top button on her blouse, undid it and began a struggle with the next one.

"Let me," she said.

He shook his head. "No, I want to."

He managed to undo all the buttons and slip the blouse from her shoulders. Then he unzipped her skirt and let it fall to the floor with the blouse. With controlled fingers, he reached under the waistband of her panty hose and pulled them down over her hips.

Nora dropped onto the bed as David knelt in front of her and slowly peeled the stockings down each leg and over her feet. Then, before he could stop himself, he enclosed her waist with his arms and put his head in her lap, his lips against the wisp of nylon panties that covered the dark triangle between her legs.

Reaching up, he touched her breasts, covered by a lacy bra, and searched for the clasp. Once again he stopped himself. "No," he muttered, "I want you to put on the gown," knowing that if he took off the last two strips of clothing that covered her, he'd never give her the chance to put on the gown. And he wanted desperately to see her in it.

"Nora," he whispered, handing her the gown, which had long since fallen to the floor, "please put it on for me."

Silently she moved away from the bed and slipped into his bathroom. She must have known, he thought, watching her disappear, that she needed to be out of his sight when she put it on.

Only a moment passed before she reappeared, standing in the doorway with the soft light from behind her creating an aureole around her dark, shiny hair. But this time it wasn't her hair that held his gaze or even her beautiful face. It was her figure in the red gown. The satiny top clung to the curves of her breasts, outlining their fullness and showing the taut buds of her nipples. The tiny straps disappeared over her soft rounded shoulders, and the scarlet diaphanous material flowed over her hips and down her long legs to the floor. She seemed engulfed by flame. She *was* a flame that burned in his heart like a beacon.

He had thought she might be shy, but she wasn't. She looked at him proudly and provocatively as if she knew how much she pleased him. "Do you like it?" she asked.

Suddenly he was the one who was shy. Or maybe he was so overcome by her that he couldn't answer. His mouth was dry. He ran his tongue over his lips and answered hoarsely, "Yes."

Nora walked toward him across the room, moving with languid grace, her steps silent on the thick carpet, her hips swaying naturally but with such a lovely effect that once more he was unable to speak.

Before he could touch her, she said, "Now it's my turn to undress you." His hand had already reached for the buttons of his shirt, but she caught it and moved it away. Her fingers were sure and quick. In seconds she'd taken off his shirt and was running her hands up the flat planes and hard lines of his chest.

"You're beautiful, David," she said, laying her head against the dark hair matted on his chest as her hands worked their way downward.

He heard her breath catch when she unbuttoned his jeans and reached inside, grasping his manhood in her hand. His own breath caught in his throat for the thousandth time that night. He couldn't wait any longer; his desire was maddening.

David pulled off the rest of his clothes and took her in his arms, holding her against him as his whole body palpitated in its need for her. "I love you," he said, over and over again, burying his face in her hair, kissing her neck, her eyes, her forehead, finally her mouth. He'd seen enough of the gown, and with eager fingers he gathered a handful of the fiery material and pulled it up and over her head.

She stood before him totally nude, and he thought his heart would explode at the sight of her. It wasn't the first time he'd seen her long, elegant body unclothed—he remembered every moment of their night together in New Orleans—but it was just as exciting to look at her now, to reach out and touch her now, as it had been before. David had the feeling that every time with Nora would seem like the first time.

Her breasts were wonderfully round with budlike nipples that called out to be caressed. With a little moan he leaned forward and touched one rose-pink tip with his tongue. She trembled beneath him, and that was almost more than he could stand. He thought he heard her speaking, telling him that she loved him and wanted him, but he wasn't sure. She may have only thought the words. They were so much in tune that he could have read her thoughts at that moment.

David lifted her in his arms and placed her on the bed. He stood there for no more than a split second, looking down at her before he knelt above her and watched as her legs opened and she rose to meet him. Never had two people been as eager to become one. Never, he thought, had a joining been as perfect. Each gave, each received, in complete accord, not wanting the wonder to end, the wonder of becoming one.

And somehow it didn't end, for when their physical joining was over, once they'd attained the heights of passion and were lying quietly with their arms around each other, they were still as one.

They were silent for a long time, holding each other, not speaking, just breathing in unison, raggedly at first and finally with ease.

"I don't think anything could be more perfect," Nora said at last, "than this, being with you."

"Each time it'll be even better," David told her, "because we'll love each other more."

Nora leaned over and kissed him then. "You've changed my life, David," she said softly as her lips touched his, moved away and touched them again.

David had never felt happier or more in love. Nothing would ever come between them, he promised himself. This would be for life. He ran his hands over her soft skin, which was so familiar and yet still so wondrous to him.

"Umm," he heard her murmur, followed by a little whisper of words he couldn't quite catch.

"What, Nora?"

"I was just thinking about my life. First you and then my father. So much good in such a short time." She rested her cheek against David's shoulder. "Maybe I'm denying his illness, but Phillip seems better. He really does."

David pulled her closer, and a little frown of irritation crossed his face. He tried to shake off the feeling, but he couldn't. Phillip was intruding even here. David had tried to put Nora's father out of his mind. That was obviously impossible. He was her father, and she loved him. That's why it was so difficult to decide what to do about the phone call from Paris.

David looked down at Nora, her dark hair spread like a cloud over the pillow. Her profile was classical in its purity. That was the outer Nora, cool and strong. Few knew the inner Nora, who was less serene, even a little unsure, vulnerable and easy to hurt. He wouldn't let anyone hurt her, not ever again.

He decided then and there that he wasn't going to tell her what he'd learned. He would handle it himself, protect her from hurt, from the truth about her father.

"David?" She was looking at him quizzically. "Now it's my turn to ask. What are you thinking about?"

"About you," he answered truthfully, "and how much I love you." Then something else occurred to him. "And oh, yes, about my mother."

"Your mother?"

"Yep. I was wondering if I've let her special spaghetti sauce burn!"

Their feet hit the floor at the same time, but Nora was in the kitchen first. When David got there, she was standing at the counter with one hand behind her back.

"Da—vid," she drawled.

"Yes, my love?" He went over to the huge pot, lifted the top and began to stir the sauce with a wooden spoon.

"Is this really your mother's homemade recipe?"

"It's what we always ate at my house. Just smell that marvelous aroma."

Nora sniffed obediently, but she was grinning from ear to ear as she held up the empty jar of prepared spaghetti sauce. "So your mother is Mama Sophie?"

David replaced the lid and tried not to laugh. "Well," he said evasively, "does it smell delicious or not?"

"It smells delicious," Nora admitted, "but I repeat the question—"

David held up his hand. He was beginning to laugh. "I didn't say my mother cooked it— I said we always ate it at my house. When you meet her you'll realize that she likes to cook about as much as—"

"You do?"

"Or?" he countered.

"As I do," Nora admitted. "She sounds like someone I'd enjoy."

"Yes," David said. "My parents are both very down-to-earth people. I think you'll like them." He leaned back on the counter, more serious now. "They haven't had an easy life, but fortunately I've been able to make things better for them in recent years. They have a nice home now, and you'll be very welcome there, Nora." Then, less seriously, he added, "But my mother can't cook."

Nora saw that he was trying to lighten the mood again, and she joined in. "How about your Dad?"

"Nope. Can't cook, either. They've made it that way for forty years." After a moment he added, "I don't see why we can't do the same, do you?"

Nora's eyes widened, and a deep flush came to her cheeks. "No," she said, "I don't see why we can't."

"I'M GLAD you could make it, Phillip," David said.

The two men were once again at David's club, but in midafternoon there were no members to overhear laughter. In fact, there was no laughter, and David was determined to keep it that way. He planned to get right to the point, not giving Phillip a chance to go off on one of his tangents. But if Phillip had any idea of the plan he wasn't cooperating.

"Happy to join you, David. This club reminds me of one in London where I've spent more hours than I'd like to admit, over some of the world's best brandy. Did I tell you about Lord Marchmont's club?"

"No, you didn't, Phillip," came the answer as David searched for a way to get to the subject that he wanted—and dreaded—to approach.

"Well, I guess I was too carried away by the Biarritz plan," Phillip responded. "I'm ready to get going on it anytime you say the word."

Evasively David answered, "I would think you already had a new career, working with Nora." He was unable to keep the tinge of sarcasm out of his voice. Phillip didn't seem to notice, but David knew the older man had a way of avoiding the unpleasant.

"I enjoy working with my daughter, but it's her business, really. She's just humoring an old man, a dying old man."

David felt the muscles in his jaw clench convulsively. "So your health is no better? I thought Nora told me you were in remission."

Again Phillip avoided the innuendo. "Yes, I am, and doing very well, too. However, one never recovers. One only hopes to keep busy in the short time allotted. That's why I thought the Biarritz project would be important for me to undertake. Keep me occupied, you know," he went on, a little shakily, David thought, as if he were beginning to see that he wasn't on very solid ground.

David took a big swig of his drink, and the instant he set his glass down with a resounding thud, he knew he'd made up his mind. "Let's cut out the bull, Phillip. I've been in touch with friends in Paris."

"Oh?" Phillip adjusted his cravat and raised one dark eyebrow. Otherwise his expression didn't change.

David had to hand it to the older man—he was a cool individual. He could probably stand before the guillotine without blinking an eye, sure that he'd be able to talk his way out of execution. Well, he wasn't going to talk himself out of this.

"I know all about you, Phillip. I know that you ran out of money and friends in Europe. I know you were left without a place to turn to and came back to Nora seeking refuge."

Phillip's hand was steady as he lit his cigar. His voice was calm as he answered. "David, I can't imagine what you're talking about. Naturally I had enemies, people who were jealous."

"Jealous, hell." David tried not to explode, forcing the words out through clenched teeth. "They wanted your neck. I imagine they were fed up with all the big deals that came to nothing."

"Really, dear boy," Phillip objected, his voice talking on a British inflection that he must have thought elevated him above all this.

"Oh, for God's sake, Phillip, I don't care about your schemes or the enemies they produced. All I care about is the ruse you've pulled on Nora. No one in Paris, not even your most recent lady friend, knew anything about this fatal disease. You've managed to keep Nora away from your doctor, but I may just call him myself."

Phillip was silent.

David, righteous in his anger, went on. "There is no doctor, no illness. It's just another scam, but this is one I *do* object to, and I object strenuously, because it involves living off Nora and taking advantage of her."

Phillip's eyes were wide, and there was resignation written on his face. "You've done your homework thoroughly, David. I should have realized you were enough in love with Nora to look after her. I admire that."

"We're talking about you, not me," David retorted sharply.

"There is a physician, by the way," Phillip corrected. "There just isn't any disease, at least not a serious one. And you're right, I left Paris because I had to, and I came to Nora because there was nowhere else to turn."

David didn't voice what he was thinking, that he would gladly kill Phillip if it would help Nora in any way. He limited himself to saying, "This is going to hurt her terribly. She's grown so fond of you, and when she finds out how you've lied—" David couldn't even finish the sentence. He didn't know the extent to which Nora would be affected. He only knew she would be hurt, and he'd taken it upon himself to keep that from ever happening again.

"I know," Phillip said. His sadness was genuine. "I've really messed up, haven't I?"

"That," David said with a bitter laugh, "is an understatement, but I'll tell you one thing, Phillip. I'm going to be there when you tell her the truth."

Phillip looked fixedly at his half-empty glass, not meeting David's eyes. "How can I do that, David? I've always loved her, of course. She is my child, but it's an abstract love. I came to her out of desperation because I needed a little time, a breather, before going out among the wheelers and dealers again."

"Time and money. That's why you jumped into Keepsakes with both feet."

"Yes," Phillip admitted. "I knew I could help with the business, and I did help, David, but I also knew that I wouldn't stay with it. I have trouble sticking to projects, especially ones like Keepsakes. It's not big enough, not dangerous enough."

"Not unsure enough," David added.

"All my schemes haven't failed, David," Phillip said sharply. "I've earned big money in my time." Then he stopped himself, embarrassed that he was bragging at such a moment. "None of that matters now."

"No, it certainly doesn't."

"What matters is the pain I've caused my daughter. You see, David, I didn't know that my love would change from the abstract to something very real. I never thought I would care for her so much and find such happiness." There was a catch in Phillip's voice that seemed real to David, but he wouldn't let himself believe Phillip capable of any true emotion.

"She thinks you're dying, Phillip," David reminded him. "What were you planning to do when the death-bed scene never materialized?"

"I don't know. I never thought that far, because I wasn't planning to stay that long. But I suddenly had a daughter, and we were both enjoying ourselves. I'd become a father again at my advanced age. That's a very singular experience, David."

"I'm sure." David wasn't sympathetic.

"It could still work, David. Medical records are full of miraculous recoveries—"

"No," David said adamantly. "Your daughter may love you, Phillip, but she's not a fool."

"I want to stay—she wants me to stay."

"Not your way. Tell her the truth, Phillip, with no more tricks. Start out straight with her this time. She'll respect you for that."

"No, I can't." Phillip's face suddenly looked old and haggard. His hands were shaking.

"Why not? Are you afraid to admit you've been a charlatan?"

"Yes," Phillip answered honestly. "She looks up to me now. In her eyes I'm a good person. I don't want her ever to know the truth."

"You can't just run away," David said, but as he spoke the words he knew that might be the solution.

"Yes, I can," Phillip said. "I'm an expert at that. I'll just disappear from her life."

"It will hurt her," David said hesitantly. After all, that might just be the solution.

"Of course, and she'll miss me, but you'll be there to help her through it. She'll have wonderful memories of a loving father, and she'll never know how I've lied to her. Don't tell her, David. Never let her know." There was desperation in his voice.

David was silent.

"Swear to it, David."

Finally the answer came. "I swear."

"Good," Phillip said. "I can trust you."

"You'll need money." David reached for his checkbook.

"No." The response was firm. "I've saved my commissions, and they're honestly earned. I haven't stolen from my daughter, and I'm not going to take from you. This time I'll do it on my own."

Now that how to deal with Phillip had been decided, David knew this was the best for Nora. He would take care of her.

10

SUNDAY WAS NORA'S favorite day of the week. She would usually sleep late, read the *New York Times* and then, if the weather was good, take a walk through the park over to the East Side to visit one of her favorite museums. Since Phillip had come to live with her, she'd enjoyed her Sundays even more. Listening to him dissect the newspaper, commenting in his inimitable fashion on theater openings and society parties, had become one of the highlights of the day.

The evenings belonged to her and David. Occasionally Phillip joined them for dinner, but he always managed to disappear early, leaving them alone together. They laughed over Phillip's excuses as he departed, which ranged from a date with a lady friend to getting his beauty sleep. There was no doubt about it—Phillip Chase had become indispensable in her life.

Nora had no reason to believe this Sunday wouldn't be like all the others. After putting the coffee on to perk, she dressed warmly in jeans, a sweater and a down jacket for the two-block walk to get the *Times*. As she was paying for her paper, Nora decided it would be an even better day if David joined them for his favorite French croissants and brioches.

She walked an extra few blocks to the bakery, even though she knew her trip would be greatly delayed by a long conversation with the proprietor, who opened up early on Sunday mornings to cater to the whims of West Siders like Nora.

She arrived back at her apartment laden with the breads, her cheeks pinkened by the autumn chill.

"Phillip," she called out as she headed for the kitchen, "I'm back." Nora dropped everything on the butcher block table and turned off the coffee, which she judged was now probably too strong to drink. "Phillip, the coffee's more than ready," she called again, "and the *Times* weighs about six pounds. Let's get into it!"

When she heard no answer, Nora went back to Phillip's room, chatting to him along the way, "I bought out the bakery this morning and decided to ask David to join us." She knocked on the door. "Let's have a cup of coffee first. It's strong enough to wake the dead."

Still there was no answer. Nora knocked again. "Phillip?" She was suddenly worried, aware that he could be ill . . . even— Nora didn't allow herself to finish that thought as she pushed the door open and walked in.

He wasn't there, and at first she felt a sense of great relief, thinking he must have awakened early and gone for a walk, which would be unusual but possible. She let herself enjoy that thought for a long moment before reality took over and she forced herself to look at the room.

The bed was made up with a blanket folded at the foot, the curtains were pulled back, the ashtray was spotless. The room looked just as it had the day before he'd moved in. Neat, clean—and empty. There was no sign of his silk bathrobe, which usually hung on the back of the door. No sign of the silver comb and brush that were always on the bureau. Almost in a trance, Nora walked across to the closet and opened it. His clothes were gone. She tried to think, to make herself understand what this meant. And then she saw the note on the bedside table.

"GO OVER IT ALL AGAIN, Janice," Nora ordered. "What did he talk about on Friday? Did he make any plans? Did he mention leaving? Think, Janice. Think."

"I am, Nora, and I can't remember anything out of the ordinary."

Janice had been summoned by an urgent call from Nora. Without changing from her funky Sunday morning outfit, she'd rushed to Keepsakes, read Phillip's note and sat still for Nora's interrogation. Janice hadn't been able to shed any light on the mystery of Phillip's disappearance.

"He acted the same as always, Nora. You know, nice and friendly and outgoing. He talked with old Dr. Irving, who's broken up with one woman and found himself another. They're taking a trip, and he wanted Phillip to find something appropriate. I believe they settled on some kind of diary for her to record their travels in. I'm not sure but—"

"Janice, get back to Phillip," Nora said, frustrated.

"I'm trying to, Nora. He talked to clients and told me stories and made *fajitas* for lunch. It was just like any other day with your father."

"How did he act?"

Janice thought for a moment. "Normal," she said. "Happy. Nora, he was the same as always," she insisted.

"Nothing else?" Nora prompted.

"Not a thing," Janice said. "You know I would tell you. I want you to get to the bottom of this, too."

Janice was saved from further questions by the sound of the doorbell. She disappeared down the hall to answer it.

David rushed into the room, removing his coat. "I'm so sorry I wasn't there when you called, Nora." He crossed the room and took her in his arms, holding her close, protectively. "I had to go into the office this morning, and I just got back and picked up the message on my machine."

"Oh, David, I'm so glad you're here." She let herself be comforted in his arms.

"What is it, Nora? You sounded frantic. What's happened?"

Janice had quietly disappeared into the back of the apartment, and Nora remained for a moment in the comfort of David's arms before answering.

"It's Phillip," she said. She was still holding the note she'd found on his bedside table. She handed it to David.

He stepped back, glad for something to focus on so that he didn't have to look at her face. He knew what was in the note. Quickly his eyes scanned the lines.

My darling Nora,
This is the best way for us to end a wonderful interlude in my life, and I hope in yours. I've been truly happy for the first time in years. I'm so proud of you and can only think of what a credit you are to your mother. I see the best of her in you.

Isn't it fitting for us to say au revoir now while the memories are so good? Please let these past weeks be what you remember of me. I will never forget them.

Be happy and don't worry. I carry your love with me.

Your loving father

David took a deep breath and gave the note back to Nora. Phillip had been deliberately vague, and maybe that was for the best. On the other hand, his farewell note raised more questions than it answered, and it was answers that Nora wanted.

"What do you think it means, David? Where is he?" Tears glistened in her eyes, and behind the tears he saw fear and pain. Once more he took her in his arms and held her close, promising himself, as he'd promised Phillip, that he would take care of everything.

"I don't know where your father is," he said. At least that was true. Phillip had divulged none of his plans.

"But it seems obvious that he feels right about leaving, and he wants you to feel the same."

"How can I feel right about something that's so *wrong*, David?" Nora looked up at him with eyes that begged for an answer to her question.

Unable to provide one, David tried to reassure her. "More than anything, Phillip wants you to be happy, not to worry."

"Not to worry?" Nora broke away and began to move around the room. "How can I help but worry when he's out there alone?"

David had gone over this conversation many times in his mind, and in his mind he'd always been able to make Nora understand. Now he was beginning to realize that she might not be capable of understanding at this point. He tried another tack.

"He *wants* to be alone. Otherwise he never would have left."

"Nonsense," Nora blurted out, startling David with her fervor.

David crossed to her and put his hands firmly on her shoulders. Clearly he would have to take control now, and she would have to listen.

"Nora, stop and think. This could be Phillip's way of sparing you pain, by going away and leaving you with only good memories. It's what he wants, Nora. You must respect that."

"It must mean that he's dying, David. He wants to spare me that."

David put his arms around her again and didn't answer, relieved that she let herself be held.

"I don't want him to die alone." The tears that had glittered in her eyes spilled down her cheeks. David could feel them through the fabric of his shirt. They were almost too much for him to bear.

"I don't even know who his doctor is," she said suddenly, panic in her voice. "I should have made him tell me. I should have made him tell me everything. If he's had a relapse—"

"He doesn't say anything about that, Nora, and he's certainly smart enough to seek medical help if he needs it. It could be that he just felt it was time to go, to move on." Even as he spoke the words, David knew they sounded weak and hollow, hardly convincing.

Nora didn't even seem to be listening. "What will he do for money?" she asked suddenly.

"He'll get by, Nora. He always has. Besides, he has his commissions from Keepsakes."

"That wouldn't last him very long, not the way he spends."

"If I know Phillip, he'll come up with a scheme," David told her, smiling and hoping for a smile in return.

It didn't come. Her face looked so terribly sad, so far from smiles that David felt an ache inside just looking at her. How it hurt him to see Nora in pain, especially when he'd contributed to it.

He'd helped Phillip devise a plan to leave town, and now he was caught up in Phillip's web of deception. He'd known all along that he would have to lie to Nora, but he hadn't thought about how devastating that would be for them both. Phillip had come to Nora with a lie—his very presence was a lie. Now there was no way out. It was too late for the truth.

David's only hope was for Nora to do as her father asked, keep the good memories in her heart and get on with her life. It was for the best. David had to keep telling himself that, knowing that someday in the future when he told her—and he would tell her—she would agree. Until then, he had to protect her.

David had been listening as Nora tried to control her sobs, and when she was quiet, leaning against him, he kissed her cheek softly and said, "You love Phillip, and he loves you. This is the best way, Nora. Please accept that."

"I don't think I can, David," she murmured against his shoulder.

"I'm here for you, Nora." Holding her even closer, David hoped that somehow he could transfer strength to her, the strength to get through this ordeal. "I love you," he whispered, "and I'll take care of you."

Nora raised her tear-stained face to look up at him. "I love you, too, David. I couldn't make it without you, but Phillip is my father, and I want him with me. I can't bear to lose him again without knowing why."

"That may be your only choice," David said soberly. "You haven't the slightest idea where he is."

"I know," she said with a resignation that made David relax a little, but only until she seemed to recoup her strength. "I must try to find him, David. I don't want him to die alone."

Nora was convinced her father had gone away to die, and David couldn't tell her otherwise. He couldn't tell her anything. All he could do was try to convince her that a search for her father would be hopeless. David, who had talked large corporations into doing as he wished, certainly should be able to keep the woman he loved from locating her recalcitrant father. And yet, when it came to strength, Nora probably possessed more than the governing board of any corporation. But this was a battle David had to win. For Nora to uncover the truth would bring her even more pain.

BUT NORA HAD DEVISED a plan, and knowing she was going against David's wishes, she'd waited until he'd left to put it into action. It hadn't taken long. Using her own intuition and working with the best private detective agency in New York, she'd been successful. Now for the second time in weeks, she was flying back to New Orleans, but this time for very different reasons. Instead of running from her father, she was pursuing him.

It hadn't taken long for the agency to find out that Phillip was in New Orleans, ensconced in one of the city's most expensive hotels. That hadn't surprised Nora. In fact, it made perfect sense that Phillip would go home to his roots, home to die, and that he would spend his last penny to do it in style.

Nora hoped she wasn't too late. Even this short delay, she told herself, was partly her fault. She should have insisted on finding out the name of her father's doctor. If necessary, she should have searched out a specialist, the best physician available, to help her father.

She'd made a mistake, but she wouldn't make any more. She vowed to bring Phillip home with her, back to New York, where he could get the best possible treatment. She vowed to save him; she wouldn't let Phillip die.

Less than an hour after her plane landed, Nora was knocking on the door of her father's suite at the Royal Orleans. She waited for what seemed an inordinate amount of time before he answered. And in that time, panic set in. She felt herself gasping for breath, afraid that the end had already come and she was too late.

When Phillip opened the door, Nora breathed an audible sigh of relief, not noticing that he looked as healthy as ever, dressed in his maroon silk robe and ascot, the ever-present cigar clenched between his teeth. He barely had time to remove it before she threw herself into his arms.

Nora saw the look of astonishment on his face, but she didn't see the other look that he managed to hide until she was enveloped in his bear hug.

"Phillip," she said shakily, "what in the world is going on? I've been frantic. Are you all right?"

"Of course, I am, Nora." He detached himself and looked down at her, one hand smoothing back a lock of her hair. "But I'm a little perturbed at you. I told you not to look for me."

"I had to. I was so worried, but I'm not worried anymore. It's going to be all right, because I understand everything now."

"Everything?" Phillip turned away and headed for the bar in the corner of the room.

"Everything," Nora affirmed. "I know you left because you're ill and don't want to burden me. But you could never be a burden, Phillip," she said lovingly. "You should know that by now." Nora found herself smiling with the knowledge that they were together again. "We'll fight this damned illness, and we'll win. I won't lose you this time," she said staunchly. "Not without one hell of a battle."

Phillip still hadn't turned to look at her. With a hand that shook visibly, he poured a stiff drink. Nora waited, knowing that what he was going to tell her would be traumatic, girding herself for the worst and sure that she could bear it.

At last he turned and looked at her. "Oh, my dear, I wish you hadn't come. I wanted to spare you this."

"I don't want to be spared. We're family. I want us to be together."

Phillip took a huge gulp of his drink and stood looking wonderingly at her. Then he shook his head as if in amazement. "What did I ever do to deserve you, Nora?"

"This has nothing to do with deserving. It has to do with loving," she countered.

"I do love you," Phillip said simply.

"I know that, and I love you."

"I just hope your love is strong enough to understand what I'm about to tell you."

Something in the tone of his voice made her look up sharply.

"Maybe you should have a drink, too, Nora," he offered.

She shook her head, watching while Phillip finished his drink and poured another. There was a look on his face that she'd never seen before. If she hadn't known better, she would have called it fear, but her father had never shown fear in his life. Even the knowledge that his life was ending hadn't frightened him. Then what could the look mean?

"You know," he said almost conversationally, "I could make up a spiel to tell you. I'm good at that. You'd probably believe me, and we could buy a little more time together."

"We'll have lots of time," Nora said, still not understanding.

"I hope so," Phillip said almost sadly.

"Oh, Phillip," Nora said. She felt herself go weak and sank onto a love seat in the living room of his suite, thinking that the end must be very near.

"No, Nora," he said quickly, "it's not what you suspect, so please don't feel sorry for me. I'm nothing but a charlatan. Well, you've always known that, but I'm also a liar." He managed a chuckle. "I suppose you've known that, too, but what you haven't known is that I've been lying to you."

"I don't understand."

Phillip didn't clarify that remark right away. For a moment he seemed to be talking to himself, not to his daughter. "Yes, I lied, and now I'm going to tell the truth. If I'm able." He sipped his drink more slowly. He seemed to be making a decision at last. "The truth will hurt, Nora. It'll hurt us both, but I think it's time your old dad grew up at last."

Nora felt as if her heart would explode. The dread of whatever he was going to say was much worse than knowing could ever be. "Please," she begged, "tell me what's going on."

"All right, Nora, in simple words I never was sick. There is no illness."

For a moment Nora felt a great spasm of relief pass through her body. He was all right! He wasn't going to die! "Thank God," she said, sighing. "But why didn't you tell me in New York? Why did you—"

Phillip didn't acknowledge her expression of relief or her questions. He continued. "I was down on my luck in Europe. I had no prospects, and I was getting old with nowhere to go. I wanted to see you—that was no lie. But I also needed somewhere to go until I could restore my fortunes. I knew you probably wouldn't take me in unless I had a good story." He shrugged. "So I invented the illness."

Nora still hadn't let everything sink in. She refused to believe that what they'd had was built on a lie. "But the doctor . . ." she said weakly.

"Oh, there's a doctor, all right. There's even an illness, several of them, in fact, all related to my years of debauchery, and none of them life threatening."

"But you said . . ." Finally it all came together, and Nora knew she'd been duped. All the love, all the caring, had been a part of his perverse plan to find someone to take him in. She wanted to run, but she couldn't move. She felt paralyzed.

"Everything we had was based on a lie," she said. Her lips barely moved. She was like a statue.

"It started with a lie. Then I realized how much I cared for you, how much I'd missed you all those years."

Nora didn't even hear that. "I was easy, wasn't I?" she asked, the pain etching lines in her face and radiating from her eyes, which focused steadily on him. "Easy and gullible."

"No, my dear," Phillip said softly. "You were loving and kind. What we had together as father and daughter was no lie. It's the only truth left in my life."

Nora brushed that away, despising even to hear the word "truth" on his lips. "Tell me the rest. Why did you decide to leave? You had a good deal going, a place to live, a job, a cut of Keepsakes." Cynicism colored her words.

"I left because I had no choice and because I was a coward. I couldn't tell you. I was afraid to let you see me as I really am."

"You could have carried on the ruse," she said bitterly.

"No, my dear, I couldn't. I'd been found out."

It took only an instant for her to assimilate those words and their meaning. "Someone discovered that you weren't ill?"

"Yes," Phillip answered simply.

"It was David," she said. "Of course David knew the truth and didn't tell me, either." She felt as though a sharp knife were turning slowly inside her.

"He couldn't bear to see you hurt. He wanted to protect you and take care of you."

"Take care of me," Nora said with a bitter laugh. "Oh, he did that, all right. I suppose it was his idea for you to leave." She knew the answer, but she dreaded hearing it.

"Let's say we came to that decision together. But he didn't know I was coming to New Orleans. I really didn't plan it. It just seemed right and natural, and I thought maybe—" his eyes were filled with hope and longing "—just maybe my daughter might come after me, and if you did, then I might have the courage to tell you the truth."

Nora got to her feet. "Well, I came, Phillip, and I've heard all that I can *bear* to." At last she'd found the strength to move, and move she did, walking across the room and out the door. She heard nothing, not even Phillip's voice calling her back.

Nora wanted to hide, to run away. But she couldn't run. She had to go back to New York and get on with her life. It would be a life without Phillip and David— that much was certain. She'd opened her heart and mind to them, and they'd betrayed her in ways she never could have imagined.

No, she couldn't run, but she could do the next best thing. She could close her mind to what had happened. Arguments, excuses, apologies from either Phillip or David would be useless. There was no reason to rehash any of it. It was over. Phillip knew that now, David would know it soon. Their actions had eliminated any need for words.

To her surprise, Nora managed to sleep for a couple of hours on the flight home. Before the plane made its final approach into La Guardia, she went into the rest room, took off the last vestiges of makeup and scrubbed her face. She flashed a smile at the reflection in the mirror and told herself she looked young and fresh, not at all like a woman who'd just been through a terrible ordeal. But deep in her heart she knew that the reflection lied. She'd promised herself to forget it all, not to think about what had happened, not to analyze it or ever discuss it again. But that wasn't going to be possible. In fact, Nora wondered if she'd ever stop thinking about it and about Phillip and David, her father and the man she'd loved.

She'd ended everything with Phillip. He wasn't dying. He was well and able to go on with his life, but he'd go on with it alone. She'd closed him out forever. Now she'd have to see it properly ended with David. How she was going to do that, Nora didn't know.

David solved the problem for her. He was at the airport, standing just inside her gate, the first person she saw when she got off the plane.

He took her arm and walked along beside her. There'd been no greeting—obviously he'd interpreted the unwelcoming look on her face. She hadn't planned to see him like this so soon, but as usual, he was still in charge. It would be the last time, Nora told herself firmly.

She asked him almost without interest, "How did you know I'd be on this plane?"

"Janice said you'd gone to New Orleans. I've met every returning flight."

"You knew I'd found Phillip?" Again there was a dullness in her voice.

"I guessed that you must have."

Nora was silent as they walked along toward the terminal. David had tried to carry her small bag for her, but Nora held fast.

"I suppose Phillip told you everything."

Nora didn't answer. There was no need.

"I can explain, Nora."

She quickened her pace. The airport was busy at this time of night. Flights were announced every few minutes. Arriving and departing passengers rushed by them purposefully. Nora felt much less purposeful. Dodging the crowd, she moved to the side of the corridor and stopped. He'd forced this upon her; she might as well have her say now.

"I thought you'd changed, David."

"I have changed," he vowed.

Nora shook her head. "You're still the spoiled, arrogant man I first met. You still think you can control everything—everyone."

"Nora—"

She wasn't ready to listen. "As long as your selfishness didn't affect me, I could convince myself that it wasn't real. Then you tried to control *my* life."

David didn't even attempt to object this time.

"You went behind my back to investigate my father. I suppose it never occurred to you to tell me what you were doing?"

"I wanted to tell you, Nora. But I was afraid of hurting you."

"Did you ever consider what I wanted, what I needed? Well, I'll tell you, David," Nora said, picking up her bag and starting to walk on toward the terminal. "I needed to know the truth, to handle the situation with my father—not to have you solve it for me. You promised never to try to control my life."

"Yes, I did," David admitted, "and I knew you would resent my interference."

"You were right about that," Nora agreed bitterly.

"I had hoped your father was on the up and up. When I found out he'd been lying, I didn't have the heart to tell you."

Nora had kept up a hurried pace, and for a moment they were separated by the crowd. Then she felt his hand on her arm. "Don't you understand, Nora? You were so happy with Phillip, like a little girl enjoying her first Christmas. I couldn't take that away from you."

"So you sent Phillip away to save me?"

"To leave you some memories. Damn it, Nora, from the very beginning you talked about your lack of memories. You had no keepsakes of your own. Lord knows, it was a constant refrain. Phillip and I wanted to leave you something."

"You did that, all right. You left me bitterness and lies and deceit."

They took the escalator down into the terminal, and Nora headed for the street. "You taught me a valuable lesson, David, never to leave myself open to love, cer-

tainly not to trust." She stopped long enough to take a
deep breath and look up at him. "Now it's over, and I
can get on with my life. I was fine before you and Phillip came along. I can be the same again."

Nora started toward the door, but David moved
ahead to block her way. "It's not as simple as that,
Nora. You can't just walk out of my life the way you
walk out of this terminal."

"Yes, I can," she retorted. "And I am."

He reached out and took her arm again. "Not until
you listen to me." Nora tried to pull away, but he held
fast. She struggled more violently, anger building in her
eyes. David released his hold.

He didn't want to fight with her, and yet he wasn't
going to let her walk away without hearing what he had
to say. She owed him that much.

Nora had pushed through the door and was walking
toward the line of taxis that waited at the curb. "Nora,"
he called after her, "you're right about one thing." She
paused for a moment, almost ready to listen. "We were
both cowards, your father and I. He should have stayed
with you, and I should have encouraged him to tell the
truth. But love kept him from it."

"Love?" Nora started to dispute that, but this time
David refused to let her finish.

"He came to you out of necessity, Nora. He left you
out of love."

Nora had opened the cab door, but she didn't get in.
She just stood there, staring at David, trying to under-

stand. He closed the door for her. There was a bench next to the terminal. It was empty, and he led her to it.

"Phillip loves you just as I do, and he couldn't bear to tell you he was less of a man than you imagined. You'd forgiven him once. He was afraid you wouldn't forgive him again."

Nora sat down on the cement bench. "Do I seem so unfeeling and callous?" she asked, "that he was *afraid* to tell me the truth?" Something in the way she said the word made David realize she was listening to him now, really hearing him.

"No, my darling Nora, you aren't unfeeling. You have very high standards, though. We all want to live up to them, but there are times when it's not possible. Then you have to throw them away and let your heart take over."

She glanced sharply at him. "I did that, and look what it led to."

This was it, David thought, his chance. Either he convinced her now or she would walk out of his life forever. What he was about to say was risky, but he thought it was the truth, and only the truth mattered now. He took a deep breath and plunged ahead.

"Your love had conditions on it, Nora. You loved Phillip, but only if he was the perfect father. As for me, I had to prove myself. I was used to being in control—it was a way of life for me. I changed for you, Nora. You helped me do that, and I'm grateful. Then I slipped. Badly, I admit, but it was a mistake, not a crime. I'm still the same man you once loved, and I still love you.

I have my faults—so does Phillip. Do we have to be perfect for you to love us?"

The tears brimmed in her eyes. "No," she said, suddenly moved by his words, "you don't."

"Then let us back into your life, Nora, with all our imperfections."

"I'm not perfect, either," she said slowly. "I've made lots of mistakes, David." The tears glittered brightly in her eyes. "I'm the one who's been afraid, afraid to love without conditions, not ever wanting to get hurt."

"But you were hurt, and I'm so sorry." He touched her face gently.

The anger had left her, but confusion remained. "Will I ever be able to trust again?" There was a plea in her voice.

"Yes, Nora. I can promise you that, because we've all changed. Love has changed us."

"I don't want to lose you, David, and I don't want to lose my father."

David felt a sigh go through his body. "You won't lose us. We've faced the worst and come through. We don't have to be afraid anymore. Just accept me as I am. When I'm with you I'm the best I can be."

"Maybe we can learn to bring out the best in each other."

"We can, Nora, we can. I'll never let you down again."

Nora's kiss told David she believed in him again and always would.

All around them in the cold night, travelers waited impatiently for buses and taxis. Nora and David didn't notice. Once again they were in their own world, lost in a kiss that sealed their future.

Epilogue

BUSINESS WAS BRISK at Miss Lila's Fancy, the newest and most chic antique shop in the French Quarter. While Phillip waited on the last customer, who'd lingered well after closing time, David and Nora remained in the back office. She sat on the one comfortable chair among a disarray of table legs and assorted furniture left-overs. David perched on the edge of Phillip's desk.

"Here we are in New Orleans to visit your father and check on our investment, and Phillip spends all his time with customers."

"Have you been bored?"

"Hardly," David answered with a sly grin. "A week-end with you at the Petite Auberge more than makes up for any disappointment over Phillip's busy schedule. In fact, if he's not back here in exactly five minutes, we're returning to the hotel to take up where we left off. You remember where that was, don't you?" he asked, lifting one eyebrow wickedly.

"I remember every detail," Nora responded with a honeyed voice and answering smile. "But let's give him more than five minutes, David. After all, we should be pleased by his enthusiasm."

"True," David admitted. "Letting him manage the Fancy was a great idea."

"Even though I offered him a part of Keepsakes."

"New Orleans is his home. His friends are here, and now that he's getting older and a little more mellow, your father's happy here."

"Which reminds me," Nora said, "there's a card on the desk from Miss Lila. Phillip thought you'd get a kick out of it."

David scanned the card and smiled. "So she's enjoying the cruise to Rio. Even taking samba lessons. Lila's obviously gotten a great deal of enjoyment out of letting go of her belongings so Phillip could open the shop. He was right on target when he approached her about Miss Lila's Fancy."

"Even though I warned her against it," Nora remembered. "I thought she'd be bereft without her antiques. I guess that's just another example of expecting others to live by my rules, eh?"

"Some of your rules, I like," David said lightly. "Such as sleeping in a double bed, and sleeping until noon on Sunday."

"What about sharing the cooking?"

"Cooking?"

"Well, taking turns ordering from the deli."

"The secret of a happy marriage."

"Absolutely." She got up and put her arms around him. "And I have been excruciatingly happy married to you for every moment of these—" she stopped to think "—six months and four days."

He kissed her on the tip of the nose. "Even in my imperfect state?"

"Let's just say we're learning together." This time Nora kissed him thoroughly on the mouth. "There is one thing I've learned for sure," she murmured thoughtfully, snuggling against his shoulder. "The only kind of keepsake that matters is being with the person you love."

"Now and forever," David answered softly as he returned his wife's kiss.

Harlequin Temptation

COMING NEXT MONTH

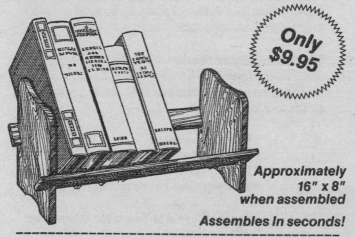

Temptation™

TEMPTATION WILL BE
EVEN HARDER TO RESIST...

In September, Temptation is presenting a sophisticated new face to the world. A fresh look that truly brings Harlequin's most intimate romances into focus.

What's more, all-time favorite authors Barbara Delinsky, Rita Clay Estrada, Jayne Ann Krentz and Vicki Lewis Thompson will join forces to help us celebrate. The result? A very special quartet of Temptations...

- **Four striking covers**
- **Four stellar authors**
- **Four sensual love stories**
- **Four variations on one spellbinding theme**

All in one great month! Give in to Temptation in September.

TDESIGN-1